Reflected in the Rain

A novel by

Alexis Anne

Copyright © 2014 Alexis Sykes

ISBN-10: 0615960782
ISBN-13: 978-0615960784

Cover design by Kari Ayasha of
Cover to Cover Designs
Edited by: Nathan Sykes

Manufactured in the United States of America

For more information visit: alexisannebooks.com

To my family~
for dragging me out of hiding, standing behind me, and teaching me every single day what love looks like.

Alexis Anne

Chapter 1

~Eve~

"You are not wearing that," I stated flatly, shaking my head and putting my fists on my naked hips.

Jake's eyebrows shot up in surprise as he stepped out of our closet. "And what exactly do you suggest I wear instead?"

I thought about it for a moment before blurting out the only thing that came to mind. "An orange prison jumpsuit."

He burst out laughing and snuck his arm around my waist, kissing my neck up and down while he ground his hips against mine. He wasn't wearing anything special—just my favorite dark wash blue jeans and my favorite tight, black t-shirt that showed off his tan skin, green eyes, and that fantastic body of his. He looked hot and I knew every single woman who saw him all night long was going to see the same thing. When he added in that casual nonchalance he had about life, Jake was irresistible.

For some reason, I could just picture Greg taking him to a strip club and getting a private room. I could see Jake all casually sitting in a booth with one leg propped up on his knee and his long arm resting along the back of the booth. I could see that bored, uninterested stare.

"Darlin', you have nothing to worry about." His lips kissed the spot behind my ear that made my knees weak and I gasped as I was suddenly, completely, turned on.

"Want a quick present before you leave?" I gasped as his hand palmed my ass and jerked my body against his.

He pulled back just enough to look down into my eyes. "Maybe. But only if it's because you're horny.

I squirmed under his intense gaze. "It's not you, Jake. I promise. It's this ritual. It just seems so silly..." I was well aware I was being jealous and irrational. I mean seriously, the man came back for me after ten years. Of course he was mine, every bit as much as I was his. I knew Jake had eyes only for me—it was actually one of the few things I believed in without question. But that didn't stop me from feeling jealous when he looked like *that*.

He laughed and pulled me onto the corner of the bed beside him. "Babe." His green eyes searched all of mine. He didn't need to say anything else but I appreciated the way his hands wove up into my hair and the intense way his eyes were making love to me. It almost pushed away the feelings of jealousy.

Almost.

"Have fun tonight. Just not too much fun," I grumbled.

Jake kissed the tip of my nose and then my mouth—we made out like teenagers for a minute before he pulled away gasping. "Fuck, Eve. Only you..." I knew exactly what he meant. How could just kissing be so much fun? "Go get dressed, woman."

I hopped up and curtsied playfully. "Yes, sir."

My hair and makeup were already done. I even had on my jewelry. I just needed to slip into my dress. But it wasn't until I looked into the mirror that I realized how sexy the dress was. It didn't seem that way on the rack yesterday, it almost looked classy. Black and shiny, but skin tight. With our crazy schedules I didn't have time to try it on until now... turns out "black, shiny, and skin tight" was also very low cut and hit all my curves in just the right ways that my breasts looked bigger and hips looked sexier than normal.

My hair was down in long, loose waves and my makeup was dark and seductive. I looked good. I just wished it was Jake and I going out together like this so we could actually enjoy being dressed up.

As I stepped out of the bathroom, Jake's eyes widened and his jaw flexed. "Nope. Not happening." He pointed at the closet. "Pick out something else."

I popped out my hip and tossed my hair over my shoulder. "And what exactly do you suggest I wear instead?" I was mocking him and Jake didn't find it

3

nearly as amusing as I did.

He glared at me and his nostrils flared. "Do not go there. I do not look like you!"

I laughed. "You're kidding right? This," I waved my hands from my head to my knees, "is exactly like that." I did the same thing to his outfit. "A sexy black dress is the male equivalent of what you are wearing, Jake."

He opened his mouth to argue, then stopped. "Really?"

I nodded and drank in the sight of him again. He'd added a shiny silver watch to his wrist and black shoes. Hot didn't even begin to describe him.

"Well, fuck! What do we do now? Because you are *not* going out like that. Not without me on your arm. Or wrapped around you. *Fuck.*"

I sauntered across the room, wiggling my hips and breasts as I walked. "I have a proposition for you."

He raised an eyebrow and followed me with his eyes. He was trying to look angry and skeptical, but it wasn't working. I could see he was both intrigued and turned on.

"We have," I grabbed his wrist and held up his watch so I could read it, "thirty minutes until our rides arrive. I will let you strip me out of this dress if you let me peel you out of your clothes and wrap my mouth around your cock."

He was breathing harder now as his eyes wandered over my breasts. "And we both pick out new outfits?"

I nodded, sliding my fingers under his shirt and

against his warm skin. "Deal?"

He didn't answer me right away. Instead he kept staring at me with a faraway look. I was starting to wonder if he was going to answer me when his eyes darted up to mine. "Tonight doesn't mean anything. And our wedding is only a formality, you know that right?" His hand tightened on my hip and his gaze sharpened. "There is no one else for me but you. I'm already married to you in my mind."

"I know," I whispered, taking his face in my hands. He had a little bit of stubble and it was rough against my palm. I wanted to feel the bite of that stubble between my thighs. "You know I feel the same way, right?" Sometimes, in the midst of my own happiness, I forgot that inside Jake there were still some past insecurities that occasionally bubbled to the surface.

He nodded slowly, but I felt like my words somehow fell short. "I could get 'Property of Jake' tattooed somewhere," I offered dramatically.

He rolled his eyes and licked his lips, his eyes zeroing in on mine for a kiss. "Don't be ridiculous," he murmured before kissing me so softly it took my breath away. He kissed me again and again, taking more of my breath with him each time. "Let's have some fun before the cavalry arrives and pulls us apart."

"Deal," I whispered as I tugged at the hem of his shirt and he let me slide it over his head. He didn't fight me when I moved to the button of his jeans. He just watched me, silently and intently.

I slid his pants and boxers down enough to release my prize—his mostly erect and perfectly gorgeous cock. I wanted to pleasure him in a way I knew he liked and make him feel good.

As I knelt down and wrapped my hand around the base of his cock, Jake brushed my hair back from my face, running his fingers against my scalp. When I looked up at him, his eyes were deep and dark, but soft.

I took it as a good sign and I smiled mischievously (the way he liked so much) and licked up his length in one long movement. Jake could barely keep his eyes open. As I wrapped my lips around him, sliding down as far as I could, my lips meeting my hand, I swirled my tongue and slowly eased back to his tip.

I paid special attention to the head of his cock until his fingers tightened in my hair. It was his sign he was ready for more, which I gave him. More than usual, actually. I don't know what came over me. Maybe it was all the weird emotions floating around us, or maybe I was just being the possessive girlfriend. Whatever it was, I was a bit more wild than normal, taking him deeper into my throat than I typically found comfortable, and moving with an enthusiasm I usually reserved for special occasions, like this.

Jake seemed to like it. *A lot.* He was moaning and grunting, sucking air in through his teeth as his hands massaged my scalp. I knew he was close by the strain of his jaw and flex of his forearms, so I reached up to cup his balls at the exact same moment I moaned. His eyes shot open, looking right into mine, and he came hard. I was a little shocked by how hard he came. I guess we were both feeling a lot.

As he panted and swallowed, he ran his hands through my hair one last time, and then bent forward to rest his forehead on the top of my head. "Goddamnit, Eve. I'm not going to be able to stand tonight." He was still gasping for air.

I smiled, "Good."

"You are evil."

I didn't act like a jealous girlfriend very often so I was going to give myself some latitude for one night. "Now, what do you want me to wear? A clown suit? Perhaps a snowsuit?"

He chuckled and tilted my head up for a kiss. "But it's your turn, babe. Get your ass up here so I can enjoy taking this dress off you."

The minute I was on my feet, Jake slid his hands up the back of my thighs under my skirt. "Damn woman, there's barely anything between you and this dress."

"We only have fifteen minutes... you better hurry or your won't have enough time."

Jake scoffed at me and stood up. "I don't need fifteen minutes, darlin'. Trust me."

Oh my. Jake was in a much better mood. He moved around behind me, pushing my hair over my right shoulder and tipping my head to the side. His hands ran up my arms and over my shoulders. "The view from here is spectacular. This is a damn fine dress, Eve."

I leaned back against his shoulder and let him peel one sleeve down my arm, popping out my naked breast. "I love that you never wear a bra."

"I know..." I breathed as he cupped me in his palm. It was warm and felt so nice.

Jake wrapped his other arm around my chest and held me against him so I could keep my balance when he started to tease me. He rolled my exposed nipple between his fingers and I gasped because it felt so good. My panties were already damp, but now they were soaking as my body warmed and throbbed for more of everything. It always surprised me, I could be so satisfied, but the moment Jake went to work on my body, suddenly I needed more. It was like I could never get enough of him.

He moved my head to his other shoulder, "Just relax, darlin'," he whispered in my ear. His left hand continued to work my nipple while his right hand caressed the fabric of my dress, looking for my other nipple. It instantly hardened under his touch and Jake ran his thumb back and forth until I was panting and writhing against him.

My body was hot and slick and so ready to combust it wasn't even funny.

"See?" he whispered in my ear. His breath was hot against the sensitive skin of my ear and neck. It tickled in a good way and only turned me on more. "I know you. I know what you need and when you need it."

He eased down the zipper on my dress and peeled it away from my skin. It slid away, onto the floor, leaving me in nothing but my utterly useless panties and Jake's hands.

"You are so turned on you're shaking, Eve." He was breathing almost as hard as I was.

"Only you can do this to me," I murmured.

He sucked in a deep breath and squeezed my body against him harder. "Fuck, Eve. If you only understood what you do to *me*."

His left hand continued to work my left nipple while his right hand slid down my belly and between my legs, stopping to rub slow, magical circles around my clit. I bucked against him and moaned as I saw stars for a second. Then he moved down to my sex, his fingers swirling and dipping beneath my soaked panties.

"Oh, you've got to be kidding me," he gasped. "You are so turned on for me... I wish we had more time." He slid first one, then two fingers inside me and I shuddered. "You stay right where you are until I'm done with you," he growled as my body contracted around his fingers.

I adjusted my feet under me, pressing myself further into Jake's chest, as he rolled my nipple in rhythm with his fingers inside me.

My undoing was the words he whispered in my ear. His lips were pressed high up on my neck as he said, "You are so beautiful, darling. I love you."

Orgasms that powerful should be illegal.

Chapter 2
-Jake-

"Eve will be down in a minute," I said as Jennie burst through the front door flushed and excited.

She looked me up and down and cocked an eyebrow. "You two are ridiculous."

"How is that?" I asked. She couldn't possibly know Eve's delay was my fault. Even though it was.

She folded her arms over her chest and scoffed. "I'm willing to bet money those pink cheeks of yours are not from running down the stairs to meet me. Also, I'm not an idiot. You two are easier to predict than afternoon thunderstorms in summer."

"Well, there could be worse things to be known for. Where's Andrew?"

Jennie flitted around me in her skin-tight black pants and shimmering gold blouse, and into the kitchen just as Andrew stepped through the front door wearing jeans and a casual white button-up with the sleeves rolled to his elbows. "What's up groom-to-be?" We shook hands and followed Jennie into the kitchen. She was already mixing herself a rum and coke. I knew she'd lived here for, well, *forever*, but it still felt weird every time she acted like she *still* lived here.

This was my house now. Not hers.

Aside from redecorating the bedroom and moving my office into Jennie's old bedroom, nothing else in the house had changed. There was no obvious mark that screamed my name when I walked through the door. Jennie could go to any cabinet and find anything.

I was seriously considering rearranging the cabinets just to throw her for a loop.

"What's going on?" Andrew asked as he watched her with about as much confusion as I was feeling.

I liked Andrew. We got along really well and even though he was a bit more uptight than I was used to, he was a good guy. Which was good since Eve and Jennie were practically one person.

"Eve and Jake were still doing it when we got here, so I'm making a drink."

"Nice," Andrew said, clapping me on the back.

"It is beyond me why any of you care about my sex life," I muttered.

Jennie just giggled and Andrew leaned against the bar stool. "Dude, we all have sex. We're glad you two are so *happy*, but sometimes we get tired of waiting around for you two."

"Are we so bad that it is actually a *thing*?" I groaned.

Jennie snorted again as she tasted her drink. Andrew looked at me pointedly and nodded. "But I don't blame you. If Jennie had a thing for public places and last minute sex, I'd be right there with you. But she has *other* preferences, shall we say?"

Jennie actually blushed. I didn't think it was possible, but her cheeks were as red as tomatoes. "Shut up, Andrew, or you aren't getting any of those *preferences* tonight!"

Before I got an unwanted dose of knowledge on Jennie and Andrew's sex life, I changed the subject. "What are we doing tonight? Why is all of this such a big mystery?"

I got blank looks from both of them as if I were the idiot in the room. Andrew broke first. "You and Eve are difficult to pin down. We all felt it was best to take away any ammunition from the two of you. You can't shoot down what you don't know about."

Well, fuck. They did have a point. As it was, I'd barely kept Eve off me upstairs. "Fine," I grumbled. "But I take no responsibility if Eve decides to kick your ass."

Jennie shrugged, "I can take her."

"Alright, let's get this over with!" Eve slammed her purse down onto the counter looking about as flushed as I imagined I did. She looked gorgeous. Her dark hair was freshly brushed and restyled after I so thoroughly ruined her earlier look. She was now dressed in a purple sequined strapless dress and her favorite black high heels. She still looked sexy (it was pretty much impossible for her to be anything else) but at least she didn't look like sex-on-heels anymore. That black dress had been... well, hot. The minute she stepped out of the bathroom my brain had gone haywire.

I walked around Andrew and slid behind my fiancée, kissing her behind the ear. "Hey darlin'."

She smiled and swooned just like she always did. "You ready for this?"

I squeezed her around the waist and kissed her again. "I want you to have fun, *just not too much fun.*" I repeated her words from earlier.

"Oh for fucks sake!" Jennie exclaimed. "Let's get going! I have two party buses full of drunks waiting for their guests of honor."

Outside, two black buses with darkly tinted windows were parked on each side of the driveway. Jennie pranced toward the one on the left while Andrew wandered toward the one on the right. After I locked the front door, I pulled Eve against me for one last kiss. She melted her body against mine and tilted her head up expectantly.

I wanted to kiss her all night. I wanted to do nothing but kiss her for the rest of time. It sounded like such a stupid thing, but kissing Eve was magic. Obviously I loved doing more, but it always began and ended with her kisses. I couldn't live without them.

She smiled, it was so obviously forced it made my chest ache. "Have fun, babe. I really do mean it. You don't go out with the guys enough."

I held her face in my hands and kissed her

forehead before pressing mine to the spot I just kissed. "Darlin', I go out with the guys plenty. You enjoy your night with the girls, ok? Promise?"

"Promise."

I kissed her one last time. I meant it to be quick— a sendoff—but as usual, it wasn't what happened. My quick kiss turned into a deep kiss. Her lips opened and her tongue slid along mine and I was done for. I tilted her back so I could kiss her harder, and when her little moans of pleasure vibrated against my mouth it was all I could do to stop from taking her back into the house and telling our friends to have a nice life without us—we were becoming hermits.

But then the buses started honking at us and our friends were obviously beating on the windows. "I think we better go," Eve said smiling against my lips.

I sighed and leaned her back up. "Fine."

She grabbed and kissed me one more time with mischief in her eyes. "Go have fun!"

"Yes, darlin'."

I watched as she hopped up into the bus. There were squeals and shrieks from her friends. Eve was going to have fun with her friends and that made me happy. I might not like being apart from her, but her being happy made me happy.

I stepped up into my own bus not quite sure what to expect. Any time Greg is in charge of planning things, there is probably going to be trouble.

There was heavy metal playing over the speakers and porn on the TV screens. *Typical.* Greg was presiding over the others like a game master. He had his customary bottle of Knob Creek in one hand and a cigar in the other.

He'd trained me in the ways of whiskey over the years and the moment he heard I was engaged, promised me an entire night of whiskey.

He was obviously not joking.

Andrew was sitting beside Ricardo. Behind them were two of our managers from work, and on the other side were two old friends of Greg's I'd hung out with from time to time.

"Hey!" they all shouted the moment I appeared.

I waved. As much as I liked and appreciated all of these guys, I wasn't particularly close to any of them other than Greg.

"Alright, alright!" Greg yelled, the cigar stuck between his teeth.

The music was lowered, though the greasy dude getting head from two giant-breasted and grunting women was still playing in the background.

"Before we get started, I'd like to present the sacrificial lamb here with his personalized bottle of the night."

The guys all clapped and hollered at me while Greg wrestled something out of a bag. When he turned around he had a bottle of Johnnie Walker Blue Label. It wasn't Greg's absolute favorite whiskey, but it was mine. And what he was holding in his hands was a two hundred dollar bottle of heaven. "I consider you a brother and I want nothing but the best for you. That includes a night of celebrating with your friends." He opened the bottle and poured me a glass. My mouth was watering just looking at the beautiful amber liquid.

"Cheers."

It was as smooth and amazing as I remembered. It burned on its way down my throat, but not like regular whiskey. This was much smoother, almost like a caress. It was like intense sex: hard and painful, but so sweet and good.

Eve was like expensive whiskey.

"You ready to have a fucking fun night of male debauchery?"

I looked over at Andrew and Ricardo who were grinning at me like I had no clue what was about to happen to me. I didn't know if I should be excited or terrified.

I took another drink.

***

With Greg in charge, anything was possible and I was prepared for every scenario. So, I was a little surprised when the bus pulled up in front of our favorite cigar bar in Ybor City. The historic district was famous for its cigar factories and had seen several transformations over the course of my lifetime. When we were in college, it was the place to party at night, but over the years, shopping, apartments, and restaurants had joined the clubs, making it an entertainment destination, day or night.

Greg and I found Cristo's Cigar Bar about a month after I moved back to Tampa and we'd been haunting it ever since. It was the perfect combination of dark wood, leather seating, low lighting, and relaxed customers. Plus, they had a ridiculous selection of cigars and whiskey.

A giant round booth in the back corner was reserved for us, and Greg shoved everyone else in first, positioning himself and me on the ends before immediately ordering Knob Creek for the table and more Johnny Walker for me. He was being more bossy than usual and I couldn't help but smile, he was so intense it was kind of touching.

A very scantily dressed (much more than usual) waitress appeared beside me with a selection of cigars Greg had preselected for the night. She quickly and deftly explained the differences between each type before turning to me. She was young and beautiful, there was no mistaking that. And I certainly couldn't ignore how hard she tried to seduce me. From the eyes to the breasts to the hips, she was giving it all she had, but I didn't give her an inch. I smiled politely and selected my cigar, getting a few snickers from the guys.

"Nice try," I said to Greg.

He grinned, "Thanks. Just doing my job, making sure you are absolutely positive you never want your hands on a different pair of breasts ever again."

"I'm good."

Greg laughed and lit his cigar, "You should be. Doesn't mean I'm not going to make damn sure, though. I don't want some mid-life crisis landing in my lap down the road." He stuck the cigar between his teeth and smacked his hands together twice. "I'm officially absolved of all responsibility. You were given your chance and you picked forever with Evie. Change your mind and I will kill you on her behalf. I don't want her going to prison over your loser ass."

I swore under my breath. "You've got to be kidding me. I can't believe you just said that." Greg was such an asshole for no apparent reason sometimes.

He leaned back in the booth, letting out a long stream of smoke. "I don't doubt you. I'm just covering all our bases. No doubts, no regrets."

I took a long drag of whiskey and turned my attention to the guys. They were deep in a conversation about the Super Bowl. It was getting heated, fast.

"How's the Gurkha?" Andrew asked.

I held it up and examined it before answering him. "Smooth. I like it. How's the Graycliff?"

Andrew let the smoke slowly waft out the side of his lips. "It's good. Greg means well, you know?"

"I know." I did. I knew he was just doing his best in the only way he knew how. Sometimes having Greg as a best friend was a blessing, but sometimes it was a curse.

No, when it came to women, it was always a curse. Greg was seriously screwed up in the head about his own love life and he used it as an excuse to tell me about mine.

Sometimes that was a great thing—he was the one who pushed me back to Tampa. He hadn't even met

Eve, but he was convinced we needed to get back together.

But other times, I wanted to punch him in the face for being an idiot.

Andrew leaned a little closer and waited for Greg to get pulled into the Super Bowl debate before speaking quietly. "There's going to be a show in about ten minutes. It's the only other crazy thing he has planned for the night. I promise."

It was the first time someone had clued me in on the plans. I nodded at Andrew to show my appreciation. I could live through a show. Hell, I might even enjoy it. We *were* supposed to be having fun, after all. Besides, I was going to need the distraction. If this was Greg's idea of a good night with the boys, what was Jennie's idea of a fun night out with the girls?

There better not be a half-naked man dancing in front of her.

Or hitting on her... I groaned and took another swig of whiskey.

Chapter 3

~Eve~

"If you don't come out, we're coming in!" Jennie called in a high-pitched voice. She was taunting me.

Jennie and the girls had rented out my favorite lingerie shop for the evening and they had given me a budget. They were helping me pick out a trunk full of lingerie to seduce my new husband, all while we sipped cocktails and ate finger foods served by incredibly hot guys.

It wasn't the worst bachelorette party in the world.

I stared at myself in the three-way mirror as pure and utter embarrassment flooded my veins. My cheeks were pink and my chest was covered in red blotches. And, yep, my hands were shaking. I couldn't believe she'd talked me into the dressing room. I was even more baffled she'd talked me into the outfit. But I was absolutely *not* stepping outside.

The curtain flung open, "Don't you have any boundaries?" I shrieked as I feebly attempted to cover my mostly naked body.

"No," she said bluntly. "This isn't any different than a bikini. Get your ass out here and show us what we're paying for!"

She grabbed me by the wrist and yanked. I really didn't have much choice but to follow her. My only other option would be to fight her off, and that just seemed ridiculous.

My friends erupted into a cheer and round of applause, followed immediately by catcalls and (what I can only describe as) devilish laughter. I turned redder. It was one thing to spend the day in a tiny bikini, it was another thing entirely to prance around in seductive lingerie in front of my friends. The clothes (or lack thereof) that I was wearing had one purpose and one purpose only: to turn Jake on. It was like they were standing in our bedroom with us.

It was creepy.

"Eve, *I* want to have sex with you in that outfit. It is damn sexy!" Sylvia was fanning herself and I would have thought she was being silly, but her eyes were absolutely transfixed.

I swallowed. "It's just your pregnancy hormones, Sylvia."

"No," our friend, Sarah, replied. She was also staring at me. "I'm definitely not pregnant and I'd definitely switch sides for you in that."

I blushed again, but relaxed a little. I was wearing a blood red and black lace bra and underwear with matching garter belt and stockings. And now that I wasn't mortally terrified of standing in front of a room full of my best friends and the waiters they'd hired to serve us for the night (dressed in only pants), I could actually enjoy what my friends were trying to do for me.

"I want to see the black corset!" Jennie crowed as she started pushing me back toward the dressing room. Then she leaned in to whisper in my ear. "Will you just relax and trust me already? Here—" she shoved another glass of champagne into my hands before she yanked the curtain closed.

Jennie was pretty pissed I didn't trust her. I really couldn't blame her. She was my best friend and I knew (hidden deep down inside) she would never do anything that would make me so uncomfortable I couldn't have fun. But everything about the night was making me nervous. Did Jake and I really need to spend a crazy night out with our friends?

Really?

Couldn't we just skip the whole "last chance to be single" and move on with our lives? Apparently not.

I wondered what Jake was doing. Jennie made me nervous but Greg? As much as I loved that man, his lack of boundaries sometimes frightened the hell out of me.

Jake and I were finally together and happy and everything was making me nervous. It still felt too new. I was constantly worried we were one step away from another disaster that would tear Jake away from me all over again. I loved him and I just wanted a chance to be *in love* with him for a while. I didn't want anything to stand in the way of that.

So, I was making little things into big things when I didn't have to.

I stripped out of the outfit, placing it carefully on the bench. Then I found the black corset Jennie wanted to see next.

My friends were all having fun, most were pretty drunk by that point, but Jennie seemed oddly sober. I spied her in the corner whispering with the shop owner and I had a feeling I was either going to love or *hate* whatever she was about to show me.

Jennie joined me in the dressing room a minute later with a box in her hands. "I've got one more surprise for you and then I promise it's smooth sailing for the rest of the night."

Smooth... *right*...

"Seriously. Don't give me that look! I'm starting to develop a complex."

"What's in the box?" I tried distracting her.

She looked down and smiled. "These are my favorite brand of panties on the planet." She opened the box to reveal five pairs of the most delicate and beautiful underwear I'd ever seen. "Jake is going to want to tear these off of you with his bare hands... *trust me.*"

Of that, I had no doubt. "Are these mine?"

She nodded and handed me the box. "You should wear some home tonight, give him a little surprise when he undresses you."

I nodded slowly as I eyed each pair. They were all a different combination of colors.

"Are you having fun?" she asked quietly.

"Yes!" I exclaimed setting the box aside. "I'm sorry I'm being skittish. It's not you, it's me." I grinned at using the standard breakup line.

Jennie pulled me down onto the bench. We were quite the pair, her in a sparkly blouse, me in a corset. "Are you sad your sisters couldn't be here?"

I shook my head. The truth was, I was kind of glad. They were my sisters, but we were all at wildly different stages of life. June was in college and Cassandra had two little ones at home. I had a feeling if they'd been there, my night would have been more dramatic and complicated. Sure I was missing two of the most important women in my life, but they'd be standing beside me when I married Jake. I didn't need them to get drunk with me while I showed off lingerie. *That* was for my silly, ridiculous, merry band of girlfriends.

"No, tonight is perfect. Just as it should be."

Jennie smiled and let out a slow breath. "Good. I can't tell you how worried I was about making you happy tonight. You and Jake both deserve a night of fun."

"When do I get to do this for you?" I asked with a wicked grin. Andrew had popped the question on New Year's Eve, but they hadn't even mentioned the idea of setting a wedding date. Yet.

Jennie shrugged. "One thing at a time. Let's get you married first. I got the ring on my finger and the man at my side. My mother will need at least a year to plan my wedding. Just don't get knocked up first."

I knew she was teasing, but I couldn't stop the

panic that hit me. *Knocked up*? "One thing at a time, remember?"

She grinned, knowing she'd successfully pushed my button. "Get dressed, we have someplace to be in an hour."

"Where are we headed next?"

She stood and shook her head at me. "Trust me, it will be fun!"

Chapter 4
-Jake-

The night ended with everyone—bachelors and bachelorettes—at Howl at the Moon, a dueling piano bar at Channelside. There was a ridiculous amount of bad singing, but overall, I'd never had so much fun drinking and listening to music with our friends. They arranged for a private limo to take Eve and I home, even though we were all of fifteen minutes from our house. So instead, I asked the driver to take us to St. Pete and back just so we could enjoy the ride over the bay. Eve fell asleep about the time we turned around and headed back toward home.

She was tucked into my side with her head on my shoulder and I could feel every deep breath she took against my chest. Sure I was drunk as hell, but I couldn't remember ever being so happy. As the limo climbed over the Howard Frankland Bridge, I looked out over the twinkling lights of Tampa and the blackness of the bay.

I'd never felt more at home in my life. For once, I

finally felt like I was where I needed to be. I mattered, I had friends, and every morning when I woke up, I had a purpose. This was the life I always wanted and it kind of scared me that it could be taken from me. Life could throw curve balls at us, I knew it would, but I couldn't lose the things that mattered. I couldn't lose Eve.

She burrowed in closer to me, as if it were possible. She was tucked so tightly into me there was nowhere else for her to go except into my lap. But I hugged her tighter anyway. I loved it when she wanted more. *I* needed more.

I knew in college she was the one for me, but all my years without her taught me just how special our love was. There were all kinds of love in the world, but what she and I had was an extra gift.

So my future was simple: love Eve with everything in me and protect us from the world.

The limo pulled up in front of our house. "Hey," I whispered, kissing the top of her head and squeezing her.

But instead of waking up, she sighed and hugged me more. God, I loved this woman.

The driver opened the door and grinned at my predicament. "Can I help you, sir? Maybe get your door open?"

"That would be great, thanks." I carefully adjusted to get the house key out of my pocket. Luckily I'd already tipped him before we left. Somehow I knew we would be too drunk and tired when we got home.

The driver took off toward the front door while I

slid across the seat with my sleeping angel. It wasn't until the cool January air hit us that she stirred at all.

"Put your arms around my neck, darlin'."

She nodded sleepily, letting her head fall against my chest as I pulled her up into my arms.

"Have a good night sir, and congratulations." The driver handed me back the key.

"Thank you, drive safely."

He nodded and jogged back off toward the open limo as I slid through our open door and kicked it closed. Eve shifted in my arms when I flicked the deadbolt.

"I love you so much," she murmured as I mounted the stairs. Every single time she said that my chest ached.

"I love you too."

She smiled and bit the corner of her lip even though her eyes were still closed. "It was a good night."

"Yes, it was," I agreed. "We have good friends."

I went straight to the bed and gently laid her down. The lights were off and the blinds were open so the room was barely lit by the street lamps outside. It cast the softest yellow glow across her face and I wanted to study her.

Watching her sleep was comforting and she had no idea how often I did it. I was afraid she'd think I was crazy watching her instead of actually sleeping, but for me it was peace.

She wasn't tainted by the world the same way I was—she could sleep at night. I watched her because she calmed me, but also because I was fascinated. What was she dreaming about? What was putting those smiles on her face?

For me, sleep was a chore. I had to sleep in order to function, so I did it. Otherwise, I'd give it up altogether. The tossing and turning weren't worth it. Neither were the nightmares.

Thankfully her dress was easy to slip off, along with her heels. But then I stopped and stared at her underwear. It wasn't what she was wearing when she left. It was a pair I'd never seen before.

They were hot. *Delicate.* They looked like they'd fall apart in my fingers and a little caveman part of my brain dared me to find out. I ran my fingers along the scalloped edge and underneath as I wondered where the hell Jennie took Eve before the piano bar.

Why was she wearing new underwear?

The more I thought about it, the more worked up I got—which was ridiculous considering she was asleep and probably hadn't done anything worth worrying about.

But I sat there stewing for a while anyway. I had to make myself get undressed, but I wound up right back on the edge of the bed watching her sleep and staring at the sexy underwear I didn't recognize.

I trusted her. Really, I did. But seriously, where had the damn underwear come from and why couldn't I stop staring at them?

I was so completely at Eve's mercy it wasn't even funny.

Damn underwear.

Chapter 5
~Eve~

Sunday was shit. We were hungover—not "college" hungover, thank god. There was no hugging of the toilet or passing out on tile floors. We slept until noon on separate sides of the bed (because who wants to cuddle when the room is spinning?) then ordered pizza. The rest of the day was made up of Gatorade and movies in bed.

Things felt off and I just assumed it was because we were both wary of asking the inevitable question: *what happened last night*? We all wouldn't have had so much fun singing at the end of the night if anyone had done anything stupid, but it was still weird. It was like asking about what happened at the doctor's office—you want to know, but at the same time, you don't. I *might* have been content to leave it alone, but Jake was acting so strangely I just couldn't.

He was a million miles away from me, both physically and mentally. He was distracted, his eyes rarely made contact with mine, and he never touched me. Not even when I sat in his lap and ruffled his hair.

"Should I be worried?" I finally asked. I was sitting cross-legged in the middle of our bed, my feet tucked up under me with Jake's ancient USF t-shirt on and not much else. I'd woken up in nothing but my new underwear.

His head jerked and he finally looked at me. "You? Why would *you* be worried?"

I loved his response because it told me everything I needed to know. There was nothing for *me* to be worried about, but clearly *he* was worried. The question was why? "You've barely said two words to me—and talking about pizza doesn't count."

His beautiful lips turned down into a frown and he looked at me pointedly. "I'm not avoiding you. I didn't do anything I regret last night. There were some very scantily clad dancers and one very pushy waitress, but that was it."

I smiled a little because of the twinkle in his eyes. "You weren't tempted out of the garden?"

He closed his eyes and shook his head, "Nope. But I think Greg was. I'm pretty sure he hooked up with the waitress before we left."

That sounded just about right.

"So why aren't you talking to me?"

Jake stewed for a minute, pulling in his lips and crossing his arms before he seemed to decide he was going to say whatever it was he had on his mind. He grabbed my ankles, pulling me across the bed and onto my back, then climbed over me and looked deeply into my eyes. It took my breath away. There were a million things going through Jake's mind and I didn't have the slightest idea about any of them. He lowered his head down and gently kissed my lips before pulling back and gliding his hand down my body, lifting the bottom of my (his) t-shirt up. His fingers slid under the very delicate fabric of my new panties and a grim look crossed his face. "I've never seen these before," he whispered.

It took my brain approximately five seconds to put two and two together. "*No.* No, no, no, no! Whatever you are thinking, just stop it!" I placed my hands on Jake's chest, but when he didn't meet my eyes again, I grabbed his face and forced his eyes away from my panties. "The girls bought us a ton of lingerie for the honeymoon. We went to Satin and Lace. We had the party there while they made me try on outfits."

He stared at me for a good ten seconds before he made any sort of movement at all. He didn't breathe or twitch, or *anything*. It was freaking me out. But then a sly smile crept across his face, turning up his eyes and popping out his dimple. "Lingerie, huh?"

I ran my fingers up into his hair and let out a very relieved sigh. "Lots of it."

Jake's mood had swung as far in the opposite direction as possible. Suddenly he was seductive and obviously turned on. "Where is all this new lingerie?"

"It should be delivered soon, actually. Would you like a private show?"

He nodded quickly. He looked like a kid on

Christmas morning, giddy and excited to open his presents.

With our little misunderstanding behind us, we decided to get in some "practice" for the honeymoon.

All in all, Sunday was a wonderfully relaxing day off.

Monday was a different story. My morning was all business, moving from meetings to planning and back again.

"Sure you want to come back after you marry Prince Charming? Don't you want to enjoy all that married life has to offer?" Carey Thomas thought he was hilarious as he leaned casually against the conference table in his black slacks, white dress shirt, and shiny red tie. He was handsome in a goofy way, his dark hair was long and little greasy for my taste, but his jaw was strong and his brown eyes were piercing.

"Oh, you never know. I may change my mind. After all, working with you is rarely worth it."

The truth was, while Carey had a crude sense of humor and always gave me a hard time, he was really good at his job.

"Aw, c'mon. Give a guy a break! Do you know how much work it is going to be while you and Joshy-poo ride off into the sunset? I'll be covering your lucky ass's non-stop. You should be nice to me!"

I chuckled as I gathered up my paperwork. Not only was I taking two and half weeks off for our wedding and honeymoon, but pretty much as soon as I returned, Josh was taking two weeks of paternity leave. We had a temp coming in to help with the hole Josh and I were leaving in the pre-season ramp-up.

"Take care of my temp and I may just have those tickets you've been begging for..."

Carey stood straight up. "Seriously? You aren't playing with me, are you?"

I could play it cool, draw things out a little longer and make Carey miserable. Or, I could dangle the bait right in front of his eyes. I slid the tickets out from the back of my folder. "Two tickets, front row center, to the Justin Timberlake concert."

He lunged for the tickets which I moved out of his reach. "Not a chance. The concert is in two months. I have them, you know I have them... I expect flawless work while I'm gone."

He looked me up and down, the eagerness written all over his face. "And I get the tickets? Promise?"

"Promise."

He stood up a little straighter. "Consider it done. Not that you had to worry, I've got your back, Daniels."

I tucked the tickets back away. "I know, but I like giving you a little incentive. You always work harder."

He groaned and started toward the door. "You know, if I didn't like you so much, I'd probably hate you."

"Get back to work, Carey."

I stood there stewing for a minute. Carey was being a jerk to get under my skin and it worked beautifully. Every time someone suggested marriage was going to change my life I wanted to scream. It seemed vowing to stand beside Jake and love him for the rest of my life somehow translated into affecting my ability to do my job, think for myself, or maintain authority. I really hoped Jake was getting teased too. That would mean it was just the normal ritualistic teasing all couples got before the wedding. But if this kept up I was going to have to set the record straight—the simple act of falling in love didn't change me.

I headed back toward my office, which took me right past Josh's. I heard his voice before I even got to the door. It was loud (which for Josh was very unusual) and he was clearly angry. I poked my head in the door.

Josh's office made mine look like a cubicle. It was nearly three times as large, with massive windows. His wood desk was situated in front of the windows, facing the doorway. Everything was dark woods or hunter greens and navy blues. It would be imposing if it weren't for the windows. Memorabilia hung from every wall and was displayed on every shelf. Josh loved signed balls and bats, and that alone took up most of his office.

He looked up and as soon as we locked eyes I knew it wasn't good news. Josh looked like he was going to rip someone's throat out. "Renegotiating the contract is not on the table. It's simply not an option. You are on the hook through the end of this season, renegotiate then." His knuckles were white as he strangled the phone in his hands.

I closed the door and moved over to the desk wondering which "contract" was in trouble. When I was beside him, Josh put the call on hold. "It's Synergy. They are trying to use a loophole in the contract to renegotiate the concert series."

"How much?" My stomach dropped a little. Our concert series was a huge part of our plan for every season, but this season in particular.

"They want a ten percent bump."

"That's not the end of the world..."

Josh shook his head, "And they want to cut the children's concert series."

I practically grabbed the phone out of Josh's hands. "They want to *what?*"

He only nodded and threw his hands in the air. "David is getting chewed out by Synergy for not getting us for more, so he's trying to throw it back on us."

"What's the loophole?" I was not going to let David's mistake become mine.

Not happening.

"We didn't specify the safety specs for the new outdoor fan experience in the contract."

"What? He's grasping at straws, give me the contract. I'll take care of this." In many ways this was my ass on the line, not Josh's. It was my fiancée who built and engineered the new fan experience, it was my new concert series, and it was my contract. If anyone was going to fix this, it was me.

I flipped to the appendix in question while Josh put us on speaker phone.

"I'm not sure why we're still talking, Josh. Talk to legal and accounting and get back to me with a new contract."

"Hi David," I said flatly.

There were some shuffling noises from the other end of the line before David replied. "Hi, Eve. I didn't realize you'd joined us on the call." David suddenly didn't sound so sure of himself. In fact, he sounded downright scared.

I loved when people were scared of me.

"Look, Josh has gotten me up to speed on things and I'm not sure what it is you are trying to do here but I will not be taking this up to legal, nor will I be asking accounting for more money."

"But..."

"No. If you look at Appendix D you will see the safety specifications you mentioned are, in fact, listed from the blueprints with a note that final specs would be provided by Spencer, Hamilton, and Associates at the completion of the project. All you have to do is request the specs."

The line was silent for a moment before David replied. "I would like to request the final specs."

"I'll have them to you by the end of business today."

"Thank you," he said flatly. "Synergy would still like to reopen discussion on the concert schedule and compensation."

"Touch my series and I'll make you pay us."

"Eve... let's be reasonable. Please? "

I rolled my eyes at Josh who was looking a little

less green.

"Be honest with me and maybe I can work with you."

By the end of the phone call, I somehow managed to finagle an extra act out of David while only giving him an extra two percent. In reality it was a win all around. David got to the number Synergy needed to hit. Which, it turned out, was the bottom line for everything. If David couldn't make their numbers work for the board of directors, there was going to be trouble for all of us. So I gave him his money in exchange for an extra act.

"If you don't mind, I'm going to go get those specs from Jake personally."

Josh chuckled and spun in his chair. "It's not going to be the same while you're gone. I'm going to miss you."

"It's going to be weird to have you gone, too. What a bizarre year we're having..."

He walked me to his office door. "A good year, though. Life moves forward, what better way to see that than weddings and babies?"

Josh was going to be a great dad. He was already hopelessly in love with his daughter. I didn't think it was possible for a man to be so excited to have a baby girl, but Josh was living proof it was possible.

"I'll see ya later, Big Daddy."

***

I didn't text Jake to let him know I was coming. I

wanted to surprise him.

I was feeling, shall we say, *feisty*.

Lisa, the receptionist, smiled as soon as I opened the doors. "What a nice surprise, Eve. You haven't been by much lately."

I leaned against her desk, "Wedding planning should come with a warning label."

"Not enjoying it?" she looked at me with sympathy.

I shook my head. "Not even a little. I love that everyone is so excited, but I just want to get married."

"Well I am very much looking forward to everything."

Greg poked his head out of his office. "I thought I heard your voice." He was dressed in a smart navy suit with his blonde hair more ruffled than normal. He looked a little ragged, actually. "We still on for lunch Wednesday?"

"Absolutely. I'm looking forward to it."

He kissed me on the cheek and winked. "We should plan something devious. Jake has it coming..."

Lisa rolled her eyes and shook her head as Greg and I jokingly plotted to keep Jake busy on our wedding day.

"Where is my groom anyway?"

"On the floor. He'll be done soon."

"I think I'll wait in his office then. You should be working, shouldn't you?"

Greg flashed his devilish smile at me, "Something like that. Have fun in Jake's office."

Oh, I was planning on it.

Chapter 6
-Jake-

"No, I'd look for an imperfection in the material. My guess is that is what keeps randomly throwing the drill off."

Jim sighed as he looked back at the machine. "Alright, I'll have it figured out by the end of the day. Thanks for taking a peek, boss."

I clapped him on the back, "No problem. You're doing great. Really, you are."

Jim smiled weakly and nodded. "Thanks for saying so, I appreciate it."

I was just about to check on my next team when Greg came bounding toward me. He had one of his ridiculous grins on his face that said more than words ever could. "You have a visitor in your office."

I wasn't expecting anyone. "Who?"

Greg ran his hand over the toolbox and shook his head, which to me was a sign I was being dense.

"She's awfully pretty."

Eve. My adrenaline kicked up just at the thought of her. She was a drug and I was a junkie. It was ridiculous and awesome. "Thanks."

"No problem. How are things coming?" He cocked his head toward the machine.

"We'll start test runs tomorrow."

"Perfect. We won't even miss you while you're off on the Dream Boat."

"Island," I corrected him.

"Fuck, whatever. While you are on a magical vacation, the little people back here in the real world will be just fine without our fearless leader."

"You sure know how to make a guy feel loved." I shook my head as I headed back toward my office.

"I love you, man!" Greg laughed as I disappeared.

Eve was twirling in my chair and flipping through my papers. "Hey, handsome." The flash of her eyes and the slight upturn of her lips made me want to kneel in front of her and bury my face between her legs.

"Hey, beautiful. To what do I owe this surprise visit?" I closed and locked the door behind me and started toward my main door.

"Don't worry, I already locked it."

My heart beat a little faster in my chest. "Well then..." I turned back toward my desk and sat in front of her, running my hands through her hair and tugging lightly.

Her eyes rolled back in her head and she sucked in a quick breath. "I did come for something specific."

"Oh?" I ran my hand down her neck and massaged the muscle of her shoulder. She relaxed and became putty in my hands.

"Mmmm.... I need the final safety specs for the fan experience. Synergy is trying to pull a fast one on me."

"I could have sent that in an email."

She smiled up at me and arched an eyebrow. It was so hot when she did that. It always made me wonder what dirty thoughts were running through her head. "True, but this way we both get an orgasm, too."

Even though I knew that was exactly what we were about to do, I still stopped breathing the moment she said it. "Working with you is very demanding."

"Wait until we're married. I only get worse."

Her hands were on my thighs and her thumb was moving closer and closer to my quickly hardening cock. "That is so hot."

Then she bit the corner of her pink lip and reached for my belt which only made the blood rushing to my cock pump harder. "No, office sex is hot."

Yes, yes it was. We'd only had sex in her office that one incredible time I'd fucked her against her desk after work. Every other time we'd done it here, in my office. It was safer and almost as much fun. And at least here we wouldn't get in trouble... I was the boss. And I'd had new locks installed on both office doors to help ensure privacy.

"It's been a few weeks, my desk was getting lonely."

"Well we certainly can't have that," she laughed, shaking her head and zipping down my fly. My brain actually turned off for a few seconds as I went sex-blind. When she did things like that—or when her fingers touched my skin—I went dumb. My cock was in control of everything.

I could spend the rest of my life analyzing it, but I would never be able to properly explain what Eve did to me. It was unique and amazing. It was an experience from my body to my mind. She turned me on completely and controlled me absolutely. Plenty of things aroused me, but nothing came close to sex with Eve.

Her voice was tantalizing, her eyes were seductive, and her breath against my skin was always my undoing. Her body was beautiful, and I was pretty sure that to me, it always would be. It spoke to me. It wasn't just how she looked but how she was shaped. I wanted to caress the curve of her hip, run my hand along the soft skin of her belly, kiss her collar-bone. Her breasts were perfect, but it wasn't about the size or shape. It was because they were hers. Her lips were mine. I loved kissing them, watching her bite them between her teeth, run them along my skin. Her tongue always made me shiver because I had no idea what she would do with it next. And her thighs... I loved to sink my fingers between them, run my own lips up the inside and smell the distinctive scent of her arousal. I loved it because it led to the one thing I craved more than anything else: being inside her.

Honestly, nothing felt like being buried inside Eve. It lit up every inch of my skin and I could feel her everywhere. I'd never felt anything else that even came close.

The moment her hand closed around my cock I knew I couldn't have a slow teasing romp with her. She gasped as I grabbed her up and pulled her against me. "Jake! What are you doing?" she was laughing and the vibration went right through me.

I pressed her against my throbbing erection and kissed her neck. "I want you, *now*."

"Oh..." she breathed and ground against me.

I smiled against her skin. "Yeah, oh. You know what you do to me..."

I curled my fingers under the hem of her skirt— God, I loved that she usually wore skirts—and slid it up her thighs. She was breathing pretty hard, her chest rising and falling so dramatically it was impossible to look at anything else. Her hair was long and hung down around her breasts which just made me stare more. As she slid her panties down, I unbuttoned her shirt and groaned.

"Fuck... the lacey black one?"

She smiled and leaned in to whisper in my ear. "Yes, the one that clasps in the *front*."

I'm not afraid to admit my hands were shaking as I reached up, making contact with her warm skin, and slid my fingers around the clasp.

The moment the bra was undone, Eve pushed me back against the desk, placing her hands on top of my shoulders and one knee on the desk beside me. I wrapped my hands around her hips and helped her straddle me as I sat back on the desk. "In a hurry?" I joked.

She pressed a finger to my lips and glared at me. "No talking. It's the middle of the work day."

I could hear the sounds of my employees hard at work on the factory floor. It was an excellent reminder that we were technically doing something rather risqué.

And it made everything so much hotter.

Eve hovered over my pulsing erection and I rearranged my boxers before grasping myself so she could take me. The moment she pressed her hot, throbbing core against my desperate cock, I saw stars. She shuddered.

How she was so wet when I'd barely done a thing would always amaze me. Maybe she was as hopelessly turned on by me as I was by her. I liked to think she was.

She took me slowly, easing around my head then taking me in inch by inch until we were locked together. Her hands were wrapped around my neck and mine were around her hips. She was on her knees on the very edge of my desk, her naked breasts in my face, and I was in heaven.

She moved up and down, faster and faster, her breathing becoming more ragged every second. Her eyes were closed and she was so close to orgasm. The closer she got, the more she fluttered around my cock. It was the most amazing sensation to feel her muscles lose control. To know she was so turned on—by me—that her body was coming undone.

I was barely holding it together. I'd been ready to come from the moment she climbed on top of me, but the pain of holding back was worth every second of work. I was not letting go until she did.

"So close," she gasped. "I'm so close."

"I know, I can feel you."

I pulled her perfect pink nipple into my mouth and sucked at the same time I slid my hand up her back so I could hold her while I used my other hand to rub her clit.

She was shaking and shuddering and—finally— coming. She clamped her lips shut to muffle her whimpers of absolute satisfaction while I watched with fascination.

Watching Eve come was a religious experience. I had each and every one of her orgasms burned into my brain for all eternity. I could live forever on my memories alone. But each new memory was a gift, and this one was no different.

"I'm going to have to remember this position," she whispered as she laid her forehead against my shoulder. "It hits all the right angles."

Uh, yeah it did. Her legs were starting to shake so I stood up with her wrapped around my waist and laid her down on top of my papers. "Your turn," she smiled sleepily.

Damn she was beautiful when she was satisfied. "Is this ok?" I asked as I thrust inside her.

She nodded and smiled, running her hands up my arms. "I'm perfect."

It took me a moment to unlock myself. All those minutes of holding back, I'd almost forgotten how to relax. But as I buried myself inside Eve over and over I lost all sense of time and place. The build-up hit me hard and all at once. It was like an arrow inside my cock, pulled back and waiting to fire. I thrust hard two more times and then buried myself deep inside while the world went white.

"Shhhh!" Eve giggled and ran her fingers through my hair as I collapsed on top of her. "You're making too much noise."

I kissed her chest and neck a dozen times. "I don't care. That was a fucking amazing orgasm. Totally worth grossing a few people out if they were stupid enough to listen."

She giggled again, running her hands along my shoulders and sighing. "True enough."

"Guess we better clean up, huh?"

Her brown eyes locked onto mine and I shuddered. When she did that, I swear she could see my soul. It was like I was always naked in front of Eve. No one else did that to me.

I stayed buried inside her while I reached into my side drawer and pulled out a box of tissues. It only took a few minutes for us to clean-up, rearrange our clothes, and share a bottle of water.

"How do you want the files?" I asked, shaking my head to clear it as I finally sat down in front of my computer.

Eve giggled mischievously. "Email?"

"I told you I could have emailed them..."

"But this was so much more fun," she whispered, climbing into my lap, making it impossible to send her the email she needed.

"How about I email it, put it on a flash drive, and print a copy?"

She kissed my cheek where she claimed I had a dimple. "Perfect. You take such good care of me."

Those words hit me hard. They weren't words I took lightly. Taking care of Eve was very, very important to me. "I try darlin'."

She kissed me again, "You do a very good job."

I looked over her shoulder as I hit the print button and then "send" on her email. "How was work today?"

"Good, weird." She stood up and returned to her bottle of water. "My meetings went well. I bribed Carey and trained my temp. Then this hiccup with Synergy happened. Everything is fine now, but it made the morning interesting. I thought Josh was going to have an aneurysm."

"He's still in 'new-dad' mode. He'll go back to being himself soon enough." Even though I rarely saw Eve's boss, I was more than aware of how his impending fatherhood had affected him. The normally quiet and well-mannered man had become a half-cocked ball of tension. Things he normally wouldn't have gotten worked up about were driving him crazy.

It made me wonder what I would be like in the same situation. Becoming a dad was a big deal. You were taking on the responsibility of raising and protecting an innocent human being. Just adding Eve to my life had permanently changed me—what would a tiny little human do to me?

"What are you thinking so hard about?"

I looked up and reminded myself we agreed to leave this discussion until after the wedding. We had enough on our plate at the moment. Kids were not something we needed to complicate matters. "Just how funny Josh can be."

Eve nodded, but I could see by the look in her eyes how little she believed me. I'd never be able to keep a secret from her, which was fine with me. But what if we wanted different things? With as tuned into each other as we were... it kind of scared me to think how something as huge as kids could affect us.

Chapter 7

~Eve~

I had Tuesday off to take care of last minute wedding details, so I was home that evening when my day suddenly took a very unexpected turn. I was wearing black leggings and one of Jake's button-up shirts over a camisole. My hair was piled up on my head and I was barefoot as I shoved another round of wedding gifts from the front door to the guest room. They'd started pouring in the moment we announced our engagement and the closer we got to the big day, the more furious the deluge of packages.

In fact, it was starting to look like we were moving. Not only were there wedding gifts, but the rest of the house was covered in wedding junk. The living room was stacked with boxes filled with our wedding favors and the coffee table was covered in seating arrangements. I'd wanted a free-for-all, but my mother insisted on assigned seating. She claimed that after a lifetime around ballplayers I should know better than to allow them to think.

Whatever.

I just wanted to get married.

The dining room table was covered in paperwork from the caterer, the baker, and the alcohol supplier... and that was just the beginning of the list. Somehow my mother had managed to invite nearly three hundred people to our small, quick wedding. Considering Jake's guest list included only ten people, I was sticking to my opinion that my mother was insane.

But then I'd remember my sister Cassandra's wedding and thank my lucky stars Mara didn't have a year to plan this. Of course Timothy's family was just as large as ours and also a baseball family. Their wedding had been insane. There was no other word for it.

There was the brawl that broke out between the Red Sox line-up and Ray's line-up. At least they'd waited until Cassandra and Timothy left... ballplayers were a special beast. Drunk ball players were impossible.

That was when my doorbell rang.

We didn't get many solicitors in our neighborhood and I wasn't expecting anyone, but the wedding gifts had been arriving constantly. I went to the door expecting yet another delivery man.

It was not a delivery man.

What greeted me stopped me dead in my tracks. It froze every muscle in my body and took my breath away. I'm pretty sure my heart stopped beating as I took in the sight of the most beautiful redheaded woman I'd ever seen in real life.

She stood expectantly on my doorstep, dressed in a beautiful gray suit that complimented her figure. Her eyes were a fascinating shade of green and her red hair fell in soft waves around her shoulders.

I knew in my gut who she was the moment I laid eyes on her.

Ashley.

She looked me up and down and shook her head with confusion, "I'm sorry, I might be in the wrong place... I thought this was Jake Spencer's house."

I would have responded if I could have found my voice, but I was frozen, absolutely stunned into silence. It was such a weird feeling that it threw me even more off than I was already feeling.

She bit her lip and looked me up and down with an expression that triggered the jealous fiancée inside me. My heart jumpstarted. "This is my house, actually. Jake is golfing but he should be home soon. Can I help you?"

It was her turn to be shocked. Those beautiful green eyes widened and her porcelain face got whiter and whiter until I was worried she might actually pass out on my doorstep.

My damn doorstep... I should put a "No Surprise Guests" sign out because this was getting ridiculous.

"I'm sorry," she finally stammered. "This was the address he sent me and I just *assumed* it was his house... that was silly of me."

"Who are you exactly?" I asked, crossing my arms

over my chest and sizing her up in a way I knew would make her even more uncomfortable than she already was. It was probably an incredibly bitchy thing for me to do... but I didn't give a crap.

She seemed to pull herself together, straightened her shoulders and stuck out her hand. "Ashley Grove. Jake and I used to work together."

I looked at her hand for a full five seconds before I slowly reached out and shook it. I really didn't want to shake hands with *her*, but some sort of polite training took over and I carefully shook her hand as if it were made of poison.

I had to physically stop myself from wiping her whore-vibes off of my hand.

But then I got to play the trump card. I liked that... probably too much.

"Eve. Daniels." I enunciated each word separately and carefully.

This time she didn't just turn pale, she visibly shrank back, her shoulders curving slightly inward. It was as if I'd just punched her in the gut.

Which I had... with two words.

Ashley slowly nodded her head and finally took a deep breath. "I see he found you, then. Good for him."

I just stared at her while I tried to decide if I should punch her in the face or full-body tackle her. Either worked for me. Punching her would be so satisfying it wasn't even funny. But a full-body tackle could lead to a nice all-out brawl and I'd really like to relieve all the tension I suddenly had built-up inside me.

Plus, I was ninety-nine percent positive I'd kick her ass.

"Yes, he found me..." I repeated back to her slowly.

"I'm happy for you both. Look, I realize I shouldn't have simply appeared on his doorstep like this regardless of his situation, but I'm here on business. You said he'll be home soon?"

It was like she flipped a switch. The stunned woman who'd just been standing in front of me suddenly transformed into a calm businesswoman. I was fascinated by how easily she did that. It was a special skill to hide your emotions so quickly and effectively. "Yes, would you like to come in and wait for him?"

Despite having just asked when Jake was coming home, she seemed thrown by my question. She stared at me before finally smiling slightly and saying, "That would be nice. Thank you."

I stood to the side and held the door open while she walked into my home. It was so wrong. Half of me was screaming, "*What are you doing, moron? Kick her ass!*" While the other half of me was calmly reassuring, "*That's it, lead her in, make her feel comfortable,* then *kick her ass*".

I closed the door. "Would you like anything to drink? A water perhaps?" See, I could totally be civilized.

"I'd love a water. Even winter here feels so hot and humid."

I snorted. It was sixty-eight degrees. It was not

hot and it was hardly humid. "Have a seat in the living room and I'll get us both a drink."

It wasn't until I was putting ice into two of my nicest glasses that I realized I'd just sent Ashley into the *living room*—as in the room covered in our wedding plans.

Oops.

When I handed her the water I saw that the cool façade she'd put on a few minutes ago was gone and the stunned, blank look was back.

"I'm sorry, I can move all of this," I said, waving my hands over the seating chart.

Her eyes flicked up to me, wide and vibrant green. They were so different from Jake's shade of green. His were warm, almost liquid. Hers were like beacons, flashing and brilliant. "You're getting married?" It was a question and a statement all in one sentence.

"On Saturday, actually."

She took a sip of her water and slowly shook her head, "I have impeccable timing, don't I?"

That was one way to put it. I sat down on the arm chair across from her and sipped from my own glass. Did I play it cool or crazy? I was fine with either, but I decided I didn't want her to know how far under my skin she'd gotten. I wanted to save that for a special occasion. "We don't leave until Thursday so whatever business it is you have with Jake can be taken care of before we get married." I liked the double meaning behind my words. Subtle, yet true.

"I can assume he's told you about me? You

seemed to recognize me from the moment you opened the door."

Damn. She was very perceptive. Very cool. She may have been thrown by finding me at the door, but she was still able to keep her wits about her enough to observe me. "Yes, I know who you are." *You are my worst nightmare.*

She swirled the ice cubes in her glass before taking another sip. "He didn't talk about you at all for the first three years we were seeing each other. Not once. He never mentioned your name or what was really making him so crazy."

I had no idea why she was telling me that, but it made my heart stop. Or maybe it was more like a knife through the heart.

She looked up from her glass. "And then something changed. *He* changed." She shook her head at the memory. "All of a sudden he couldn't stop talking about you. He was fixated and fascinated by everything about you. I thought for sure he was exaggerating, he had to be glorifying a part of his past that was actually good."

I felt like she was trying to tell me something, but all I heard were the words she'd just said, over and over in my mind.

He never mentioned me.

He changed.

He was fascinated.

That was when the front door opened and the sounds of Jake and Greg's loud, happy voices echoed through the house. I was trapped between some sort of alternate past reality and my very bizarre present. I jumped up from my seat and practically ran to the door.

Jake and Greg had played a late round of golf with two of the managers from the company as a send-off for the boss. Both men were grinning and a little red in the face from what was probably a pretty decent combination of exercise and alcohol.

Jake grabbed me up the moment he saw me, pulling me off my feet and into his arms, "Hey darlin', you look good enough to eat," he growled.

Greg swore under his breath. "Number one rule, Jake! *Not in front of me*! Number one." He held up his finger and waved in front of our faces. "Why can't you keep it straight? You two are a nonstop sex train and I can't take it anymore—" Greg stopped mid-sentence as he saw our uninvited guest. "What the *fuck* are you doing here?"

Jake shot me a confused look and slowly lowered me back to the ground. His eyes were locked onto mine with a thousand questions I couldn't answer any better than letting him see for himself. "You have a visitor," I whispered and stepped to the side.

Ashley was standing in front of the couch, facing us. She and Greg were trading not so quietly whispered insults. My love of Greg was skyrocketing by the second. I absolutely loved how much he hated *her*.

"What are you doing here?" Jake asked, confused.

Both Greg and Ashley stopped and turned to face Jake. And me, I guess. But I was pretty sure I was no longer the main event.

She straightened herself again and plastered the world's fakest smile onto her pretty face. "Hey, Jake. It's good to see you."

He ruffled his unruly hair with one hand while blindly reaching for me with the other. His fingers touched my waist, sliding along the small of my back, and curling around the other side, gently pulling me against him. "It's been... a while."

She smiled tightly and her eyes flicked down to mine. "I hear you're getting married. Congratulations."

Jake's arm tightened around me but Greg beat him to the reply. "It's "best wishes" moron. You don't say congratulations until after the wedding. It's bad luck."

Ashley and I both glared at Greg. Who was the bigger idiot now? Ashley or Greg? Because my bet was that Ashley would love to send our marriage some bad luck.

"Oh, fuck it." He waved his hands at us and threw himself into the arm chair.

"Thanks Ash," Jake finally replied.

My chest tightened. *Ash.* I could probably land a couple of good punches before Jake pulled me off of her. I knew Greg wouldn't move a muscle, so it was only Jake I had to worry about stopping me.

No one moved or said anything for a few moments and the void between us felt more like a massive black hole trying to suck us inside.

"I have good news," Ashley finally said. "That's

why I'm here... can we talk for a few minutes?"

Jake looked down at me, almost as if he were asking permission. Or maybe he was gauging my mood. He was probably freaking out inside his head. "We should sit," I offered, gesturing toward the couch.

As much as I wanted to kick her ass out of my house, I also knew I needed to be civilized.

For the moment.

He nodded and smiled, a silent conversation passing between us. One in which I assured him I was fine and he assured me that he wanted her out of our house just as fast as I did.

I sat back down in the chair I'd just vacated, and Jake sat on the arm beside me. He held my hand firmly on his leg. I certainly didn't mind that he'd chosen my left hand, or that my engagement ring was facing Ashley.

She noticed. Her eyes narrowed on the ring as she watched Jake and I settle onto the chair.

"So what is this news you traveled all the way here to surprise us with?"

She plastered that fake smile onto her face again and took a deep breath before plunging in. "Steele Industries wants to acquire The Nugget."

Jake let out a low whistle and Greg sat up straighter in his chair. Whatever The Nugget was, it had both their attention. Unfortunately, I was clueless.

"Outright?" Jake asked.

She licked her lips before speaking. I was very

aware of the way she focused solely on Jake. Ashley hadn't looked back at me once since mentioning the wedding. It was as if Greg and I no longer existed to her. And her eyes were softening, almost flirting with Jake. "Their initial offer is to purchase all rights to The Nugget and bring both of us on fulltime to finish developing it."

"Oh, hell no!" Greg said, standing up. "He's *my* partner now. You can take your offer and shove it up your ass, sweetheart."

Ashley whipped her head around so fast I thought it just might spin off her neck. "I know that, *asshole*. I was merely telling him what the initial offer was. Back off and cool your jets before you blow off your own damn balls."

I could be wrong, but I was pretty positive Greg and Ashley didn't just hate each other, they *despised* each other on an epic scale. He flicked her off and sat back down.

"Alright... now that we have our private parts under control... what is Steele really offering?" Jake looked equal parts confused and intrigued.

Ashley looked physically uncomfortable. Her hands twisted in her lap and her brow furrowed up before she spoke. "Steele wants to purchase The Nugget and bring both of us on, but they are willing to negotiate. They indicated they may be willing, if The Nugget is, in fact, what I've demonstrated, to come to a mutually beneficial compromise."

I didn't like anything I was hearing because if I was right, I was pretty sure Ashley had just said she wanted to work with Jake to sell this product. And that was not happening. Like... *ever*.

"And they would then take it and integrate it into their products, I'm assuming?"

Ashley nodded slowly and Greg just scowled at Jake. I squeezed his leg, "Could someone tell me what The Nugget is so I can at least *pretend* to follow along?"

Jake looked down at me surprised, almost as if he'd forgotten I was there. But then the blood drained from his face a little and I realized it was more than that. Jake hadn't forgotten me, he was dreading telling me something. He was all too aware of the fact I was sitting there beside him. "You remember how I made most of my money? An investment that worked out in my favor?"

I nodded, dreading where he was going with this. Jake made his money from two things: an investment, and helping design a product. I'd never asked for more information because I didn't think it mattered.

"The project I worked on was helping Ashley with a robotic sensor that Steele Industries acquired."

Ashley was the engineer he'd helped out. She was the one who'd helped Jake make enough money to invest in Spencer, Hamilton, and Associates. "Oh." It was all I could say. My mind was working too fast to stop for silly words that would more than likely only make me feel more stupid than I already felt.

I'd heard him say "she" and "her", but it never occurred to me who she might be.

Jake squeezed my hand and smiled, his eyes were searching mine with a soft and hopeful look to them. "When we were working on that project, we came up with the idea for The Nugget. It came together surprisingly quickly, but needed a lot of R&D to turn it into a viable product." He looked away from me and back to Ashley. "Which means you must have made a breakthrough of some kind."

She nodded. "I did. And Steele wants it. There is still plenty of work to be done, but it's clear now this can be turned into something great, especially with Steele."

Ashley could be turned into something great... for batting practice.

"When can we meet to discuss details?" Jake asked. I tried to pull my hand away, but he clamped down harder.

A smile pulled up at the corners of Ashley's lips. Not a large or obvious smile, but a smile nonetheless. "Does tomorrow morning work for you?"

"That should be fine." Jake replied. I involuntarily dug my nails into his leg when he said that. I didn't realize I'd done it until he flinched.

Greg shot to his feet. "Well, now that we have that all settled... your time is up. Off to your broom or hotel or whatever it is you witches use these days." He pulled on her arm and nudged her toward the front door.

Ashley sneered at Greg, "Watch it asshole. I can still bite back."

Greg laughed, "Try it sweetheart. I dare you."

"Alright, alright," Jake said. "Ash, you better go before my bulldog here loses it. I'll see you in the morning."

He pulled on my hand and I trailed him reluctantly to the front door. It was so awkward. She was probably the only other woman from Jake's past that I'd ever meet. And here she was... standing in my living room days before my wedding.

She turned at the door and smiled at me with that fake smile of hers. I just wanted to backhand it right off her pretty little face.

Damn, she brought out a surprisingly violent streak in me.

"It was good to finally meet the infamous Eve who saved Jake."

She really had a way with words. A *bad* way. "It's been an interesting evening, that's for sure," I mumbled. "Have a good night."

Chapter 8
-Jake-

We all stood there in the foyer not saying a word while we listened to the sounds of Ashley slamming her car door, starting the engine, and then (finally) driving away.

The wonderful thing about Eve was that I knew her well. The amount and type of swearing she was about to spew at me was usually proportional to exactly how she was feeling inside.

She spun toward me, her brown eyes dark and full of fire. She was fucking beautiful when she was mad. It didn't hurt that she was also wearing one of my favorite outfits: my shirt and not a whole lot else. I wanted to throw her over my shoulder, take her upstairs, and show her just how much of me she owned, to wipe any doubts or fears right out of her head.

She stuck her finger up at me and glared, "You cocksuckingmotherfuckerassholejackass! You've got to be *fucking* kidding me! Have you lost your goddamned mind?"

Eve was livid. The long string of curse words were all actions directed at me. That meant she was pissed on an epic scale at me, at Ashley, at the world... but angry Eve was easier to handle than scared Eve. I hated scared Eve because I was never sure how to handle her, and it was usually my fault, which just made me feel worse.

So angry Eve was good.

Greg chuckled, "I love how well you can swear, Eve. Really I do."

She turned her glare on him, finger pointed at him now. "You. I don't know if I love you or hate you right now. But I'd watch my balls if I were you."

He laughed some more and carefully moved his hand south until they were covered. "Yes, ma'am. Anything you say ma'am." His grin was enormous and those blue eyes of his loved how much my fiancée hated my ex-lover. Greg was thrilled to have a partner in crime. I could practically hear the gears of his brain turning. The two of them were going to be impossible to deal with until the Ashley problem blew over.

And that was only if I lived through the evening, which was very much in question at the moment.

"Don't you fucking leave the two of them alone tomorrow, you got it?"

Greg held up his free hand like he was taking a pledge, "On my honor. Trust me, you don't need to worry about that. I wouldn't leave her alone with

Jake if my life depended on it."

Now *I* glared at him. "I think it's time you found your way home. Eve and I have some things to talk about."

He made a face at me, "Have a fun evening you two. And remember, you're getting married this weekend. Don't let Miss Sunshine ruin things." He leaned in and gave Eve a kiss on the cheek. "Noon?" She smiled a little and gave him a quick hug before opening the door and pushing him out. "Noon," she agreed. "Pete and Shorty's."

He nodded, "See you then."

Eve closed the door and spun around, holding up her hand. "Don't. Just... *don't*." Then she stormed past me. The back door slammed and a minute later I heard the whir of the pitching machine around the side of the house.

Sometimes it was important to stop Eve before she got too mad, before her mind got too far down a line of crazy thoughts. But other times... it was better to give her a few minutes to let out her anger, order her thoughts, and calm down.

Every few seconds there was another chinking sound as she hit a ball. There was a net set up behind the machine to shag the balls and there were no windows on that side of the house, so I couldn't watch her. I wished I could see her face and gauge her emotions.

I'd fucked up royally. I knew that much. It was one thing to have Ashley show up, but it was another thing entirely to agree to see her the next day. To

possibly agree to *working* with her. I knew if the
shoe were on the other foot, and Sebastian was
offering to work with Eve, I'd be insane. Hell, just the
idea of it had my blood boiling.

In all honesty, I was pretty confused. This was
something Ashley and I could have easily broached
over email, or even a phone call. Why did she decide
to come all the way to Tampa and knock on my door
without any kind of warning? I was shocked when I
saw her standing there in our living room.

No, shocked wasn't good enough—I was numb. I
never, ever expected to see her again.

Ever.

To me, she was a part of a life that was dead and
gone.

I cared about The Nugget, my name was attached
to the project and the patents we'd applied for, but it
wasn't something dear to me. It was merely
something I'd leant some of my experience and
knowledge to. This was Ashley's project. I
appreciated being kept in the loop about where it was
headed but really, it didn't matter. It could sit in
computer files and on shelves unused for the rest of
time for all I cared. I certainly had no interest in
going to work for Steele Industries, and I certainly
wasn't willing to risk my relationship with Eve over a
project.

I realized Eve needed to hear all of this.

The chinking stopped as the machine most likely
ran out of balls, so I made my way outside. I
expected to get cussed out all over again, but that

wasn't what happened at all. Eve was bent over with a bucket in one hand while she tossed one ball after another inside. She was red in the face and sniffling like she was trying not to cry.

I was such an ass.

Eve wasn't a crier. It just wasn't something she did. She was very much in control of herself and liked to redirect her feelings into positive actions, like fixing problems or cussing you out. I was in deep shit if she was working this hard to keep her feelings in check.

"Eve," I said quietly so I wouldn't scare her.

She dropped the bucket and took a step back. "Stay right where you are, cowboy."

"I'm so, so sorry for what just happened in there. You have every right to be mad as hell at me."

Her face contorted, moving between unchecked rage and something that tore my heart in two.

"Stay over there," she repeated, putting her hand up.

I closed the gap between us anyway. I knew she didn't want me to come near her because it would make her cry, but I didn't care. I needed to kiss her and she needed to get mad at me. "Nope, not happening."

She tried to push me away, so I wrapped her up in my arms.

"Jake, stop! I don't want you near me right now!"

"No. I'm not moving so just stop trying."

She whimpered a little and then gave in, resting her head against my chest and finally let go. "I hate you so much right now."

I held her close to me and brushed her hair while she cried and swore at me.

"I'm sorry." The words started tumbling out of me. "I'm sorry I ever left you, I'm sorry she showed up here today, and so, so sorry I agreed to see her tomorrow. I promise, I'm just looking over the proposal and telling her I want nothing to do with any of it. I am not going to work with her. I'm not..."

Eve balled the sides of my shirt inside her fists and turned her forehead into my chest. "Why now? We're getting married, Jake."

I couldn't stand it. I grabbed her face and turned it up toward mine so I could see her eyes. I *needed* to see her eyes.

But she pulled away, scrunching her eyes shut. "Stop. Don't look at me when I'm disgusting like this."

"Fuck that," I whispered and kissed her. She was covered in tears but she was not disgusting. She'd never be disgusting to me. She fought me for a second and then gave in once she realized I wasn't kidding. She actually kissed me back a little, which was such a relief.

I pressed my forehead to hers and looked into her eyes. "I won't work with her. It will just be tomorrow morning and then I'm sending her on her way. And you," I kissed her again, pulling her up into my arms so I had one around her waist and one up her back and into her hair, "are marrying me this weekend. The only woman who matters to me is *you*. The only woman I have ever loved is you. I'm sorry I'm such an idiot sometimes."

I wanted Ashley out of my life as badly as Eve did. All I felt was dread when I thought about Ashley. The past had no place in my life.

Eve finally smiled a little. "I wanted to beat the crap out of her for coming to our house."

Hearing Eve talk helped me relax. If she was talking, she was starting to feel better, which made me feel better. "I'm actually surprised you didn't."

She grinned for a moment, but then it disappeared. "She thought this was your house. She came here expecting to find you single."

"But I'm not, so it doesn't matter," I assured her. I didn't care what Ashley thought.

Eve looked into my eyes like she was digging beneath my layers, looking inside for the answers I wasn't giving her no matter how desperately I tried. "I just thought you should understand. You're going to be with her tomorrow, so you should know what she was thinking."

"Do you want to come to work with me tomorrow? You are more than welcome to sit in on our meeting. As my wife you will have an interest in all things related to Spencer, Hamilton, and Associates. It wouldn't be weird to have you there at all. I know Greg would love it..." *Probably too much.*

She smiled again and I knew the two of them were going to be so much more trouble than I realized. "No," she shook her head. "I have plenty of work at my own job tomorrow. I trust you..."

"You just don't trust her."

"Not even a little bit."

I couldn't blame Eve. I knew if the situation were reversed I'd probably be sitting in on that meeting. I'd love to see Eve try and stop me from glaring at Sebastian the entire time. So the very fact she was feeling comfortable enough to let me handle Ashley made me feel a glimmer of hope we'd get through the next twenty-four hours without anyone being punched, maimed, or shot at.

Maybe.

"Darlin', of all the people on this planet there's only one you. I've never met anyone who drives me crazy like you do and I can't live without you. I'm not the same person without you in my life. I need you." I ran my fingers through her hair and pressed her closer to my body. "Marry me?"

She smiled and her brown eyes danced, "Do you know you've asked me to marry you fourteen times?"

I loved that she knew exactly how many times I'd proposed in the last six weeks. "And it's still not enough."

***

"They're waiting in the conference room." Lisa informed me the moment I walked in the front door. She looked skittish, which was an unusual look on Lisa. Normally she was sassy and blunt, but today she looked like she just wanted to crawl under the desk and hide.

"Is Greg in a mood?"

She rolled her eyes and tapped her pen on the desk. "To say the least. And *that woman* who is with him... she's a piece of work."

Well, that answered my next question. Ashley was already here. It baffled me how everyone seemed to see things in Ashley I couldn't. She had an uncanny ability to play me in just the right ways, manipulate me and keep me in the dark until it was too late to do anything about it. I never could figure out how or why she did it, most likely because I didn't care.

To me, Ashley was a friend I had a convenient relationship with. It served its purpose and nothing more. I was always honest and up front with her about my feelings (or rather, the lack thereof). I didn't focus on why she treated me so differently, because it didn't matter. She wasn't my girlfriend and our relationship wasn't the most important thing in the world to me. It wasn't even in the Top Ten. I cared about her as a friend... but most things concerning Ashley I just brushed aside and forgot about as soon as they happened.

It was quickly becoming clear to me that might have been a mistake. What I used to think of as a casual friendship with benefits was having a very profound effect on my life.

The most important part of my life.

Lisa held up a coffee mug. "I just cleaned this. The princess would like a cup. A little cream, no sugar."

I raised my eyebrow. "Excuse me?"

Lisa chuckled. "The first mug I gave her wasn't clean enough. I hadn't gotten up the gumption for round two, so... you get to be the lucky winner. I hear you're the reason for her visit, so, have fun with that boss."

I took the mug and shook my head. It seemed Ashley was hell bent on making my day miserable.

After gathering both her coffee and mine, I dove into the mess that was my life. Ashley was sitting at the head of the conference table. Her red hair was loose and styled over one shoulder in a soft wave. She was wearing a heavy amount of makeup with dark red lips that complimented the shade of her hair. She had on a cream pencil skirt and matching blazer that buttoned in a dozen tiny buttons up her middle. A bright blue blouse peaked out from underneath, skimming along the cream skin of her breasts. She did have a fabulous rack, not that I cared anymore.

I set the mug down in front of her. "Don't make my staff clean cups for you. It's not their job."

She smiled up at me sweetly. "I'm sorry. But it was dirty and I don't work here."

Whatever. I wasn't in the mood to start a fight over coffee, so I turned away, intentionally moving toward the seat beside Greg. "Morning."

"Morning Buttercup. How'd your night go?" Greg was playfully batting his eyelashes at me as he rested his chin on his hands like he was a silly girl interested in gossip.

"Fuck off."

That just made him grin and wink at me. "I knew you two would be all gross and in love after I left. It's just what you two crazy kids do." Greg said it loud enough so Ashley could hear.

I rolled my eyes and ignored him. The last thing I needed to do was make things any more awkward than they already were.

I set my bag down in an empty chair and picked my mug back up to swallow a few sips of the liquid caffeine. I kind of wished there was some whiskey in there. It might make dealing with Ashley a little easier.

"Alright, let's get down to business. The big boys have some real work to get back to." Greg said with a toothy grin.

Ashley sighed and grabbed a manila envelope from her bag. "Here is the paperwork. Long story short, I want, and need, to work this deal with Steele. Since you hold one of the patent rights along with me, I need to know how you want to proceed."

I glanced quickly through the paperwork. Steele was more than a little interested in The Nugget. They desperately wanted it. My best guess from some of the wording was that they had another product that would integrate with ours. Instead of developing all this technology on their own, possibly infringing on our patents, they wanted to acquire it for free use.

"Let's just sell, Ash. Why do you care about a job with them?"

I had a job, she had a job... what was the big deal?

"I want to come back to the States. I'm tired of

being a nomad and working on different contracts for different companies around the world. I'm tired of selling everything I create to the highest bidder. I want to build a life and this is a good offer."

"Have Steele buy me out while preserving the offer for you to go work for them. I don't see why they would have an issue with that."

She shrugged her shoulders. "I believe, at this juncture, they are worried about complications. They are looking for the smoothest transaction possible."

Which made sense. If they acquired The Nugget and both engineers who worked on it, they would have a pretty air-tight situation. No loose ends. But I would also happily sign away whatever rights they wanted.

"Buy me out."

She flinched a little and her jaw stiffened. "I can't."

Well, this was an interesting development. Ashley had easily made twice what I had over the years. "What do you mean *you can't*?"

She shifted in her chair and fiddled with the papers in front of her before she lifted her green eyes to mine. I saw a lot of things when I looked into her eyes, but the most obvious was sadness. Ashley was incredibly sad.

"The details of my financial situation are none of your business, beyond knowing I cannot buy you out," she said quietly. "I do not have the means to at this point in time."

I stared her down while I studied her. There was

so much she wasn't telling me. True, she was nothing more than a friend, but I did care about her. "That's all you're gonna say?"

She searched my eyes for a moment then shrugged, "You aren't the only one with a complicated past, remember?"

No, no I wasn't. There was a very good reason Ashley and I had gravitated toward each other. Troubled souls recognized each other. She recognized my fuckedupedness before we actually met. At first it had been such a relief to meet someone who understood. I never had to explain myself to Ashley—she got it because she lived it, too. Maybe that was why it was so easy to avoid conversation with her, there was just the silent understanding of who we each were and nothing more. And maybe that was why she was so good at manipulating me. One screwed-up person knew exactly how to play another screwed-up person. That was probably why I always kept her at arm's length—I knew it drove her crazy.

God, we were awful for each other.

"I have no interest in changing my position here at the company. If you want to sell The Nugget, I'm on board. Otherwise, I can't help you."

The door opened and one of our interns, Rob, stepped cautiously inside. He looked like he'd rather have walked into an actual lion's den. "I'm so sorry to interrupt your meeting. Greg, they need you in maintenance."

"I'll be there when I get there," he hissed at Rob,

who cringed.

"They said they can't wait. They need you now. It's serious." Rob was looking at his feet, and I was pretty sure he was shaking.

"Fuck nuts." Greg swore and slapped his hands down on the conference table. "Sit, Rob." The poor intern flinched and looked around at the table. Greg rolled his eyes and pointed at a specific chair right between Ashley and me. "There, in that chair. Sit there and pay attention. Don't let either of these morons move or leave, and remember every single word they say."

Rob nodded emphatically, "Yes, sir."

I sighed, "Greg, we'll be fine. You don't have to intimidate Rob." Seriously, we were all adults. He could lay off.

"Nope, I promised Evie I wouldn't leave you two alone. Rob here will fill in for me until I get back. Right Rob?" He leaned across the table, "You don't want to mess with me right?"

Rob shook his head, "No sir."

Greg nodded. "That's right. And if you think I'm bad, just *imagine* what Jake's fiancée will do to you if you fuck up."

Rob's wide eyes shot over to mine. I shrugged. Obviously no one cared what I thought in this situation.

"That's right, you know who Eve is and what she'll do to you. So just do your job son, and everyone will be fine." Greg was so dramatic. But then he turned on me. "I'll be right back."

"Go put out your fire, boss."

With one more glare in each of our directions, Greg finally left.

Rob looked down at the table. I was pretty sure he wanted to crawl *under* the table. Poor guy didn't ask to get dragged into my drama. He was just the kid who drew the short straw in the intern pool.

"Breathe, Rob. Nothing's going to happen. We're almost done here."

He glanced up and smiled a little. "Just doing my best to listen carefully."

I rolled my eyes and looked back at Ashley, "Is there anything else?" I asked.

She was sitting quietly as if she were running her options through her head. "I'm surprised. I really thought you'd at least want to see The Nugget through. It was a brilliant piece of work on your part."

A very small bit of regret flitted through the back of my mind. "Thank you."

"You used to say all you wanted to do was put good things into the world. The Nugget is good, Jake. Really good."

"I did my part. It's enough."

"Is it?" She was pushing me on purpose.

"Yes, it is. There is more to my life than a single product. I don't know if you've noticed, but I do good work here, too." I gathered the papers back together and slid the folder back across the table.

"Of course. I didn't mean to imply your work here was frivolous, but the things you and I have worked on... come on, Jake. They don't even compare. You are meant for more than a boring job making mediocre products for the American consumer."

I didn't know if I should be insulted or honored. It was a beautifully backhanded compliment. "What happened, Ash?"

She transformed so fast I would have missed it if I'd blinked. "I don't think the past ever truly leaves us alone, no matter what we do."

It was such a cryptic statement. One I hated hearing since I was betting on leaving my own past behind. "I sure as hell hope you're wrong about that." We stared at each other for a while, neither of us really willing to say anything else. It was a subject we typically avoided. The past was something neither of us needed to spend time around, no matter how much it haunted us. "Does it have to do with Charlie?"

Ashley looked out the window and took a deep breath before looking back at me. I could tell by the tension in the air my guess was right. "The short answer is yes," she said quietly. "But as I'm sure you'll understand, that barely covers it."

I could honestly say I felt really bad for Ashley. "I'm sorry to hear that."

She smiled sadly, shaking her head and looking up at the ceiling. "Nothing a little money couldn't take care of. It should get me some peace for at least a few more years." Then, in another complete about-face, Ashley smiled brightly, threw her shoulders back, and grabbed the folder off the table. "So," she drawled while putting the folder away, "if they agree to buy your rights and still take me on, you'll sign over?"

"Absolutely," I agreed as the door opened and Greg came storming back inside. Talk of the past was over. We barely talked about it to each other, so we certainly weren't going to keep talking in front of Greg.

"What are you agreeing to, Buttercup?"

"If she gets Steele to buy me out and take her on as lead engineer, I'll sign over my rights."

Greg slapped the table. "Excellent. Angel Face and I will work out the details while you're on your honeymoon. Don't worry about a thing."

Ashley glared at him. "I don't need your help, Greg. I can handle this."

"No," I interrupted. "That's a great idea. Greg knows what I want and what works. You can coordinate with him until I get back. I will be out of pocket for two weeks and you should be able to have a new proposal in hand by then."

I liked this idea a lot. It would make everyone happy. It got me out of my last tie to a past I no longer wanted, it gave Ashley the opportunity she clearly needed, and Greg was taking me out of the equation, which would make Eve very happy. Greg might even get to piss Ashley off a few times in the process. It was a win all around.

"What was the emergency?" I asked as Greg threw himself into a chair.

He scowled, "Idiot intern left the chuck in the lathe."

"What?" I practically yelled it.

"Don't worry about it. It shot straight at the wall and no one was in the way. There is, however, a beautiful dent in said wall now."

"Obviously he was one of your hires."

Greg huffed and turned to Rob who was still sitting and staring at the table. "What did they say while I was gone? Repeat it back. Word for word."

Rob stared at Greg with huge eyes. He stammered, "They talked about doing good work?"

Greg rolled his eyes and waved the boy out of the room. "I was kidding, junior. They didn't do anything stupid or say anything crazy?"

Rob shook his head.

"Good, now leave."

Rob ran away from the storm cloud that was our conference room. I wanted to join him.

Chapter 9
~Eve~

Greg and I had decided to meet from time to time for greasy food and beer in the middle of the day. Pete and Shorty's was one of Greg's favorite places to eat and we both loved the burgers. It was kind of, sort of, a halfway meeting point for us, so it worked.

I dropped into the wooden booth. There was already an order of tots and a pitcher of amber-colored beer. "Spill it. Give me the dirty details fast and hard," I ordered as I took a giant gulp of liquid heaven.

He grinned at me as he popped a tot in his mouth. He always had the most mischievous glint to his blue eyes. It made me wonder what really went on inside his head. He seemed like such a blunt, open book, but I was absolutely positive Greg was always holding back.

"It went fine. No claws were used... there *may* have been some name calling—probably on my part."

As if I had any doubt. "So far so good. Keep going." I chugged the first quarter of my beer. I'd spent the morning keeping busy with work, but I'd been tense and nervous. The idea that Jake and Ashley were talking this morning was constantly playing in the back of my mind. Beer was a relief.

"Jake told her no-deal unless it included leaving him out of it. She tried a few different angles, but your boy held his own. He did good."

"So that's it? She left and we're done?" I couldn't believe it would be that easy.

It wasn't.

Greg took another swig of his beer. "Jake told her if she could get Steele to agree to buying him out, he'd sign on the dotted line."

Crap. She was still around then. I didn't like this at all.

"Cool your jets, Evie. It's not as bad as it sounds. She's going through me." He said it like he was a proud dad, leaning back in the booth and tugging at the collar of his shirt. "Jake won't have anything to do with her until a deal is worked out. *If* a deal is worked out."

"You?"

He nodded, "Yep. It may kill me, but I'm taking point. I'll keep her off Jake and away from you. Hopefully having to go through me means she'll cut the crap and keep things simple."

Somehow I doubted that was possible. "So, what's the deal with you two?"

Greg looked away from me and concentrated on

his beer. "We're oil and water, ammonia and bleach, hydrochloric acid and... anything. We just don't get along."

I cleared my throat, "But *why*?"

He shrugged his shoulders, "Everyone has their triggers. She is each and every one of mine combined into one crazy... person," Greg grumbled. "I promised Jake I'd stop calling her names unless she really, really, *really* deserved it. He made me promise all three 'really's."

I laughed. "And some of those triggers would be?"

"Manipulative. Fake. Selfish. She tries to use her looks to get what she wants... the list goes on."

I could certainly see how they antagonized each other. Greg was a particular personality as well. As much as he and I got along, those same personality quirks would drive some women, like Ashley, up a wall. Greg was very blunt and liked real people. He loved women... *a lot*, but he hated fake women. He played with them like fish on a line.

"Ok, I can see how you two don't like each other, but it's more than that." I was getting to the bottom of this if it killed me.

He squirmed and fidgeted some more until the waitress appeared and took our orders. We both got burgers.

"Do you like her?"

He looked at me like I shot him in the gut. The complete horror showed from his eyes to the thrust of his jaw and the set of his shoulders. "No. *God, no.* No, no, no. Wash your mouth out with soap young lady."

I shrugged my shoulders, "Well, you are squirming and you two act like kids, it was one possibility."

He shuddered and chugged his beer. "No, I just..." he sighed and ran his hand through his hair. "I just don't know how much to say. Jake is like a brother to me and you've..." he actually blushed a little. The pink on his cheeks was completely foreign and kind of adorable. "You've become like a sister. I love you two to death."

I hopped up out of my side of the booth and slid in next to Greg. He lifted his arm and I ducked under to hug him. "You're like the brother I never had, Greg."

"Better than Tim?" He sounded genuinely hopeful I liked him better than my brother-in-law, then added under his breath, "Please say you like me better than Tim."

"Tim would never get into trouble with me like you. He's more like a friend. *You,* are my brother from another mother."

Greg let out a loud whooping laugh. "I'll take it."

I hoped sitting beside him, where he didn't have me staring him down from across the booth, would help him say whatever it was he was avoiding telling me. The waitress came by with a fresh pitcher and mugs. It was nice to sit so comfortably with another man I had absolutely no feelings for and no professional relationship with. Greg and I were just friends, plain and simple.

"I hate her because of the way Jake is around her." Greg said it to so quietly and calmly, it was bizarre.

I froze, his words settling around me like ice cubes.

"I don't even think he realized he was doing it, but every time she came around, he would regress. It was so weird. One day he'd be fine and dandy; joking around with everyone, happy, working hard. And the next..."

I was having a very visceral reaction to Greg's words. The last time I'd felt this nauseous was the first time Jake told me about Ashley.

"The next?" I prompted him.

"The next, he'd struggle to get through the day. Ashley seems to have a special ability to bring out the worst in Jake. And it's a two-way street. He brings out the worst in her, too."

"Greg?" He looked down at me, all big brotherly and adorable. "I fucking hate her."

He nodded and cocked his head to the side a little, "Yeah. Me too. But you know what?"

I shook my head, feeling a strange combination of sad and angry.

"You don't have a damn thing to worry about. I think the reason he hung out with her as long as he did was because he was lost. You give him purpose and direction, so it really doesn't matter that she's suddenly reappeared. She can't knock him off course like she used to."

I liked hearing that. "Greg?"

"Yeah?"

"Thanks."

Our burgers arrived and conversation veered back

toward the ridiculous. "Since the wedding ceremony isn't until five, I was thinking of sending him on a wild goose chase for most of the day. You know, making up ridiculous things you absolutely needed to get down the aisle? But then your mom yelled at me."

"Greg," I laughed, "it's an island. A *tiny* island. We're going to have enough traffic problems, please don't lose the groom."

He shrugged. "I won't. Tom and I decided we just need to hang anyway. He hasn't seen Jake in months and I haven't seen him in almost a year." A little flock of nervous butterflies took off in my stomach at the mention of Jake's uncle. I was surprisingly nervous about seeing him again after all these years.

"Good plan."

We ate some more in silence when I realized Greg was smiling and looking off into the distance. "What are you thinking about?"

His eyes snapped back to mine. "I was daydreaming. It was glorious."

"Gonna clue me in?"

He pushed around his fries before answering me. "I was kind of... maybe... dreaming about you beating the crap out of Ashley."

"So violent, Greg! I would never..."

He laughed at my lie. "Eve, you have a special place in my heart mostly because of your passion. You take no prisoners. You know what you love and you protect it without question—you are exactly what Jake needs in his life."

I kind of wanted to hug Greg again, but I stayed where I was. "Are you suggesting I am prone to fits of violence when it comes to my future husband?"

He grinned, "Heaven help anyone who comes between you and Jake."

***

My last full day of work as Eve Daniels was in the books. Thinking about Ashley all day had taken its toll on me. I felt more exhausted than usual and was practically dragging myself through the front door of our house when Jake surprised the crap out of me.

"Hey darlin', welcome home." He was standing just inside the door with an enormous grin on his face, his gorgeous dimple peeking out and his green eyes flashing.

"Thanks, baby," I replied, practically throwing myself into his arms. He was warm and strong. He was so inviting I wanted him to carry me upstairs, curl around me, and just sleep.

Instead, he took my bag from me and set it on the table.

"Take your shoes off, please."

"My shoes?" I asked, even though I was already kicking them off.

"Yep," he replied and popped his eyebrows. Jake was up to something. He looked me up and down and frowned a little. "Do you mind taking your pants off? You look too stuffy."

Now *I* frowned. "My pants? Jake, what is going

on?"

He didn't wait for me—he came right on over and reached for my waist. "Your pants, you should take them off."

Was he losing his mind? Normally he'd ask seductively, glide his fingers along my waist and kiss me until I forgot what was happening. "My pants? This can't wait until, I don't know, I get past the front door?"

He shook his head at me like I was being difficult. "Fuck it. I'll just take you like this." He bent down and threw me over his shoulder.

"What the hell are you doing?" I yelled and smacked him on the ass since I was hanging over his back. I was laughing as loud as I was yelling.

"I have a surprise for you. I was simply trying to get you comfortable, but I don't have time to waste on debates."

He took me through the kitchen and out the back door onto the porch. Our porch was wide and covered, with columns and a rail separating it from the backyard. Normally there were large, comfortable lounge chairs and tables lined up along the house, but as Jake walked me outside and tossed me down, I realized he'd rearranged everything. I landed on a mattress covered in pillows and blankets.

Beside the mattress was a table covered in a variety of snacks and appetizers. A bottle of wine was open and two glasses were waiting beside it. "We're having a picnic?"

Jake laid down on the mattress beside me, smiling

up at me as he wove his fingers up into my hair. "It is our last night at home for a while. I thought we should make it special."

"Oh," I breathed.

"Yeah, *oh*," he replied and kissed me, his tongue sliding against mine as his fingers tightened in my hair.

The weather was perfect. A cold front was sliding in from the north, so the temperature had been dropping all day. It would be raining soon and Jake knew exactly what rain did to me.

I decided I didn't want to talk or think. I just wanted to let everything go. I wanted to escape inside Jake for a little while, so I let him kiss me until my toes curled, and then I rolled on top of him.

"I think you are wearing far too many clothes, Mr. Spencer." I started at the top of his shirt, unbuttoning one after another until his shirt was open. I tugged up his white undershirt and ran my hands along the muscles of his stomach, then hooked my hand around his belt and got to work on his pants. Jake was grinning at me the whole time, his eyes rolling back in his head whenever my skin touched his.

The rain started to fall quietly, so quietly at first I barely noticed it. Not until there was enough water for it to start dripping slowly from the leaves and the roof above. It created a symphony of noises that seemed to blot out the rest of the world.

"Take your clothes off," I commanded as I stood up and finally dropped my pants. Then, with a grin, I took off my blouse and bra, but picked Jake's shirt back up and pulled it over my shoulders to keep the cold away.

"Don't you want to eat first?" he asked, grinning.

I paused as I pulled his shirt closed around my nearly naked body. "Do you really want me to stop?" I teased back.

"Oh, no," he replied with a slow shake of his head, his eyes drinking all of me in. "Get your gorgeous ass down here." He sat up and tugged on my hand, pulling me onto his lap.

I straddled him and ran my hands down his bare chest. "Who needs food when there is something this delicious in front of me?"

Jake laughed so hard he practically bucked me off of him. "Cheesy much? Get down here and kiss me, woman."

And so I did. I kissed the hell out of him. I had way too much pent up frustration from the last day. It needed a way out and Jake was my favorite way to exorcize my demons. The deeper we kissed, the more our bodies ground together and with very little separating us, we quickly moved from excited to aroused.

But the rain was falling harder and the temperature was dropping. Even with the heat generated between us, a chill ran over my skin.

"Oh no you don't," Jake grinned. Then he pulled the blankets up around us, flicking the switch on a heated blanket. "There's more where that came from if the temperature keeps dropping. I got the space heater out, but I was hoping we could get lost under all these blankets for a while, first."

Then he rolled me underneath him, "Or I could just keep you warm with me."

I liked that idea. I liked all of it, actually. The blankets were soft against my skin. I liked being lost under the covers with Jake. I never knew what was coming next... a hand, a kiss? Maybe soon he'd let me have some of that erection he had sliding against my skin.

Just the thought made my body throb with anticipation. As much as I was enjoying being lost in the blankets, nothing compared to being lost in Jake. He could wipe away my doubts and fears, quiet my mind, and relax my body like nothing else ever had or ever would. I craved the peace he gave me.

So I tilted my pelvis up and let his cock fall between my legs. I loved the way his green eyes lit up and he sucked in a breath. "Excited are we?"

I nodded and pushed my sex against him. There was an explosion of sensations from the contact of his body against mine. I wanted more so I pulled back and tilted forward again. This time he slid inside, just a little. Just enough for us both to gasp and freeze.

The rain was falling soft and steady only a few feet away from us, but we were so dry and warm under the protection of the porch. It was like we were in a bubble, just the two of us, safe together from the world. It was like Jake was feeling the exact same way I was because, just as my emotions were starting to get the better of me, he wrapped his arms all the way around my body, holding me close and locking his eyes with mine as he very slowly and teasingly started to make love to me.

With small strokes he entered me, and with each gentle thrust my body responded. I was wet and desperate for more. I writhed in his arms as my body took over—its needs and desires shut what was left of my brain down.

"I know you don't want to talk about it right now," he gasped, "but I fucking love you."

What he really meant was that Ashley didn't matter. "I fucking love you, too," I whispered, arching my back and allowing his cock to slide all the way inside me, as far as Jake could go. He was buried to the hilt and his body pressing against my clit made my core pulse.

"Nothing else feels like being buried inside you, Eve. I would live like this if we could."

My eyes were closed, my back was arched, and my hands were dug into the skin of his ass, pulling him harder and deeper every time he pulled back. I knew he wasn't actually getting deeper inside me, but I liked to think he was. I wanted us to fuse into one being.

"It might be hard to eat and watch TV and stuff like that," I gasped, then cried out as he buried himself inside me again.

"True, true..." he kissed a trail of kisses up my shoulder, gasping and pumping. "But I think I could live with the consequences."

"What if we got bored?"

Jake stopped mid-stroke and looked me in the eye, "Blasphemy. You take that back!"

Instead, I kissed him again and rocked my hips up to meet his. He groaned and pushed inside me. "Fine, say whatever you want... just don't stop doing *that*."

I nibbled at his earlobe and lower lip, "We could agree to meet at home for sex every day at lunch?"

Even that sounded too tedious. I liked the unexpected sex far too much, but I also enjoyed *any* sex with Jake, so maybe there was no such thing as too much sex.

Or maybe I was thinking way too much for someone who had a gorgeous man on top of her.

"Fuck, woman. Shut up and come."

"Sir, yes sir."

There was no more talking after that, just hands and tongues. Skin on skin. Jake inside me, and my body welcoming him again and again with every thrust, until I felt that rush of electricity sweeping through my body and coiling deep in my belly.

"Higher," I gasped. I wanted his cock to hit me right at that bundle of nerves.

"There?"

I nodded and jerked as he glided exactly where I wanted him, digging my nails into the skin of his shoulder, barely able to catch my breath as he hit that spot over and over and *over*. My whole body shook and shuddered as the orgasm detonated at the point where Jake's cock slid into my body, and washed through every inch of my skin, opening up my lungs, and making my heart race. My scalp tingled and my toes curled around his calves as I folded my body around his.

The rain drowned out my cries, not that I cared if anyone heard me.

That was a damn fine orgasm.

Jake was panting and laughing, "That felt good. Was it good?" His skin was covered in a fresh layer of sweat and my hands started sliding.

"Yes!" I breathed as he thrust deep inside me and his body made contact with my clit. "Do that again."

He grinned, his dimple showing and his eyes flashing, "Like this?" he asked, thrusting hard and deep.

I groaned, my whole body groaned. "Yes, again." He thrust over and over, I knew it was something he liked as much as I did and I was hoping in a minute we'd both be coming.

Jake grunted. The muscles of his arms straining and lifting my hips up to meet his, his jaw tightened and his eyes darkened. It was so hot to watch him work inside me. To know it was me and my body making Jake lose his mind.

He pushed inside me one last time, his cock pulsing inside me. I felt the kick and spasm, and that little movement along with his warm body pushing against my clit pushed me over the edge one last, refreshing time.

"Maybe we *should* stay like this forever," I gasped with my fingers buried in the skin of his ass.

"Because this is pretty fantastic."

Chapter 10
-Jake-

"Give me a kiss and I'll give you the grapes. It's that simple." I dangled the bunch of red seedless grapes from my fingers, letting them sway gently while I taunted Eve.

She raised an eyebrow and shrugged, "Maybe I don't want the damn grapes that bad after all."

Oh no she didn't. She was playing with me—no, mocking me. I tossed the grapes and tackled her against the mattress and pillows. She was naked and had the blankets pulled up around her for warmth. But now she had me on top of her again and I wasn't so sure two orgasms were enough for her tonight.

Not with the way she was looking. Her hair was a mess, long and dark and ridiculously tousled. It was sexy as hell as it fell over her shoulders and curled against her pale skin. When she looked like this—a combination of relaxed and sleepy and mischievous— all I wanted to do was fuck her over and over and over again.

"Are you testing me?" I growled as I buried my face in the crook of her neck. The skin from her shoulder to her ear was my favorite to kiss because she *always* let me kiss her there. And it never failed to make her putty in my hands. Sure I loved kissing her breasts, but it wasn't nearly as consistent as the neck.

And I was all about sure things when it came to Eve.

"Maybe," she gasped as my tongue hit that spot behind her ear. "Need to make sure I know what I'm getting myself into."

"What?" I pulled back so I could see her face. She was biting her lower lip to keep from giggling and her brown eyes were dancing.

"You know, before I make a life altering decision this Saturday."

I shook my head slowly with my eyes locked onto hers, "I guess I'll just have to convince you then." That was when I unleashed the tickling. I was merciless, hitting every spot I knew she hated. She laughed and wiggled beneath me, and just for the safety of my manhood, I wrapped my feet around her legs, pinning them beneath me. Then I tangled my fingers in hers, pulling her arms above her head so she couldn't move.

"Don't tickle me like this," she begged. There was real fear in her eyes.

"I'm not," I promised and kissed the hollow of her neck. Her eyes immediately softened then heated, as she realized we weren't playing games anymore.

Eve was a lot of things, but she was rarely powerless. Even when the chips were down, she found a way to turn the tables in her favor. She always managed to find solutions to every problem and keep herself from falling behind.

Except with me.

She let herself be vulnerable, she allowed me to take control, and most important of all, she trusted me.

I absolutely loved that it was something she did for me, and no one else.

So I kissed her again and again until she tried to escape my grasp. I let her go. I didn't really want to hold her down. I'd rather have her hands on me.

The second she did, I shuddered. My body reacted to her touch the same way every time. I brushed that crazy hair back from her face and looked into her eyes, "I'd never cheat on you, Eve. I can't. I'm physically incapable of sleeping with anyone but you ever again."

I kept saying the wedding was just a formality, but it wasn't. It was a big fucking deal to me. It was everything. I'd been in love with Eve for years, but I was constantly amazed by what that meant. It kept transforming into something more, something bigger. Every time I thought I could put my finger on it, and define it, my feelings for her grew deeper and I realized there was a whole other level to being in love with someone. She didn't just turn me on and I wasn't just happy when I was around her, Eve had become my life. She was everything to me and I wasn't sure I could live without her anymore.

It was crazy to think of it now, but until a few months ago (the night we fought at the hotel in Orlando) it hadn't occurred to me we could get married. But when Eve finally unloaded her anger and really let me into her mind, I finally saw everything differently. That was when I realized I meant as much to Eve as she meant to me. For some reason, up until that point, I was still convinced I loved her more. I *needed* her more than she needed me. *I* was the one at the disadvantage. She could crush me and walk away and still live her life.

But not me, I knew I couldn't live without her.

It hadn't occurred to me to ask Eve to marry me. Why would she? I would never deserve her. I wasn't good enough to love her as it was, but then I'd left her. I knew asking her to be my wife was too much.

But then she yelled and cried, and called me her *family*.

That single word meant so much to me. I saw Eve and our entire relationship differently from that moment forward. I finally realized it wasn't about deserving her—I'd never do that. But I could make her happy. My dream of building a life with her, having a future, and making our own family... it was real. It was something I could have.

I just had to have the courage to claim it.

I barely slept that night in the hotel. I wanted to ask her to marry me right then and there, but I wanted to do it right. I was going to plot and plan so

I was sure when I asked that question, the only answer I would hear was "*yes*".

My love and fidelity to Eve wasn't a question for me, and I had absolutely no doubts about her. But the act of making it official, of merging her name with mine and becoming a real family... it was a big damn deal. Ten years ago I could barely imagine a life like this, and now it was real.

"You're packed?" she asked, running her fingers through my hair. Every muscle in my body relaxed and I had to remind myself to keep from crushing her.

"Yep, bag is next to the front door and ready to go. I just need throw a couple of things in an overnight bag and I'm done." We packed two separate bags. One to get us through our wedding night, and one for the honeymoon. Packing for two and a half weeks was interesting, but it helped that we were going to the Caribbean. Packing didn't involve much more than comfortable clothes and bathing suits, even in January.

"I'm not," Eve frowned. "I'm having trouble deciding which new sexy lingerie to bring."

"That is a terrible problem to have, babe. Maybe you should model them all for me again, I can help you choose."

She rolled her eyes, but smiled. "Seriously, are you even going to care if I wear lingerie on our honeymoon?"

I'd wash her mouth out with soap if I thought I could get away with it. "How could you possibly ask that question? Are you insane? That is some seriously hot lingerie."

"Well then..." she looked me over and cocked an eyebrow, "I'll be sure to pack as much as I can. I'd love to see that face a few times on our trip."

"This one?" I asked, plastering a ridiculous smile on my face.

"Yep, that would be the one. Incredibly, undeniably, happy Jake. The most beautiful thing in the world."

I kissed her because I didn't know what to say when she said things like that. It always overwhelmed me so much I was speechless. But a kiss, a kiss I could do. So I tried to tell her how she made me feel with my lips and my tongue.

"Did you make any plans? I saw you looking at excursions the other day." I rolled to the side to take my weight off of her and rearranged the blankets. The rain was still steady. It was everything I was hoping it would be. When I heard it was going to rain all night, I pictured exactly this: us cuddled up on the porch, wrapped up naked together listening to the rain.

"No plans, but I have lots of information so we can pick and choose what we want to do every day. Or not do." She grinned and bit the corner of her lip. Eve had something very mischievous on her mind.

"What?" I asked, but she just chuckled.

"It's stupid. It's... a bad idea." She blushed. The red blotches appeared around her collar bone and streaked up to her cheeks.

"Oh no you don't." I pulled her arms away from her body and ran my hands along her soft skin. "Tell me what you're thinkin' darlin'. All your secrets are mine now, remember?" I winked so she'd know I was being playful.

When she hesitated, I started kissing her neck and nibbling at her ear, moaning and groaning until she was panting, too.

"I was just thinking... we've been so busy with getting things in order... we haven't had much... *fun* lately."

I pulled back to look into her eyes. I cocked an eyebrow. "Fun?"

She nodded slowly and attempted to bring the blanket back up around her. I stopped her. "What kind of fun?"

She blushed all over again, turning even brighter red this time. "The kind you and I like to have."

Oh.... Eve wanted to have *fun*. As in, sneak into a dark corner and let me have my wicked way with her *fun*.

"Oh..."

She smiled up at me and wiggled her eyebrows, "Yeah, *oh*."

I sat up, crossing my legs and planting my hands in my lap. I wanted to see her and really understand whatever evil idea she'd concocted. "Fill me in, I'm all ears."

She sat up too, only pulling the blanket around her waist. She fumbled around and found my shirt again, but left it hanging open so I could enjoy the sight of her breasts.

"Well, as we are both aware, you and I very much enjoy a certain high-risk level of PDA. And that PDA has been sorely missing from our lives for several weeks now. I miss it, I crave it." She blushed again. "I was thinking our honeymoon was an excellent chance to rekindle things."

My blood was pumping hard, most of it straight to my cock. I was thinking of a hundred things at once (all sexual). Places, scenarios, clothing choices... the list was overwhelming. "I like where your head is at." She still wasn't looking right at me. Her eyes were unfocused like she was thinking of something very specific in her head. "Eve, what's up?"

Her eyes darted to mine and she chewed the corner of her lip. "I may have a little game for us to try... but it could be stupid."

I was pretty sure "sex", "game", and "stupid" did not belong in the same sentence together. "Just tell me what it is. I won't laugh, if that's what you're worried about."

She licked her lips and took a deep breath. My shirt was swallowing her, the sleeves were dangling past her fingers and my collar pushed up into her hair, which was still wild and everywhere. "I was thinking we could each make a little list. Maybe wishes? Or *challenges*?" her voice dropped at the second suggestion.

"As in, I get to pick things for you to try to accomplish?" I really hoped that was what she meant, because I really liked that idea.

She nodded, "Something like that."

My cock twitched a little under the blanket. It was entering heat seeking missile mode. All these dirty thoughts of doing it with Eve all over the Caribbean were making it go haywire. "Let's do it." I already had a list a mile long.

Eve on a balcony.

Eve on the plane. Could we do it on the plane? Did people actually get away with that?

On a beach, or in the water, or on a hike...

Smoke may have been coming out of my ears at that point. The male brain can't handle that much sexual freedom all at once.

"Alright, well first we should agree to some rules."

"Rules?" I was pretty sure I had a perma-grin plastered to my face. It might not come off for a few months.

"Yes, *rules*." She rolled her eyes. She knew I was off on Fantasy Island. "Focus. We each pick challenges. They have to be attainable or it won't be any fun. And they have to be different."

"Agreed. When should I give you my challenges?"

Her eyes twinkled a little and she smiled. It was the slow sexy kind of smile that made me want to do very naughty things with her. "On our wedding day. I'll send you my list while you're waiting to marry me. It will give you something to keep your mind off selling me your soul."

I huffed, "I sold you my soul a long, long time ago, darlin'. But I wouldn't mind spending the day dreaming up ways to make your fantasies come true."

She gasped and swallowed. Apparently my words had an effect on her.

"I hope you're ready for round two, because I'm coming for you," I warned a split second before I rolled up onto my knees and prowled across the mattress. When I was over her body and looking down at her sweet lips, I stopped long enough to kiss her before I had my way with her.

Not that she minded.

Chapter 11
~Eve~

"You're doing *what*?" Jennie gasped.

We were getting pedicures. Our feet were soaking in glorious hot tubs of water while our backs were being massaged by the machines inside the black chairs we were sitting in. There was soft music playing and the sweet scent of flowers floating through the air.

Oh, and I was so relaxed I'd decided to tell my best friend about my sex ideas for my honeymoon.

Brilliant.

Not that I didn't tend to share most of my life, including my sex life, with Jennie, but I wasn't in the mood for her barrage of questions. I was even less in the mood for what was more than likely her list of ideas. Jennie's ideas were always bad. Just... *bad*. There was no other way to describe it.

"It's not that big a deal. It's just supposed to be fun. You know, make things a little more interesting."

She shook her head, rolled her eyes, and took a long drag of her wine. "Don't get me wrong, it sounds like a *lot* of fun. I'm just surprised. You and Jake don't seem like you need to spice things up."

I leaned back against the head rest as the kneading hands of the chair worked my shoulders. "I thought you had me figured out by now, Doctor Jennie. I tend to overcompensate sexually when I'm feeling vulnerable."

When she didn't answer, I looked over at her. She was leaned over the arm of her chair, her chin in her hand, concentrating. "Is this about the ex?"

Ugh. Ashley. "Probably."

"I still can't believe she showed up on your doorstep like that. What do they put in the water over there?"

"I don't know," I replied, "but it better be the last surprise to show up on my doorstep for a long, long time."

"She was really that pretty?"

I groaned and sunk further down in my chair. It didn't matter that Jake was mine. And it totally didn't matter that I was perfectly happy with my own appearance. The other woman in my man's life was pretty.

"Gorgeous. I still can't get over the hair. Who has hair that shade of red? I wanted to stare at it." No, actually, I wanted to play with it. Every once in a while I was such a girl.

Jennie flopped back in her seat and made some sort of grunting noise. "Well, Jake always did have great taste. Would it have been better or worse if she was hideous?"

Did it matter? "I think the bigger issue is what is underneath the red hair, perfect pale skin, and bright green eyes. I swear she is as different from me as possible."

"You mean she actually trusts her best friend?"

Ouch. Maybe I deserved the dig, but did it have to be while talking about Ashley? "For the millionth time... I'm sorry! My party was amazing and you did a great job. I should have trusted you. Thank you and I'm sorry."

Jennie was grinning, "I forgive you. You should know full well by now I know you inside and out. I gave you a perfect night for *you*. I expect the same courtesy when it's my turn."

"Strippers?" Strippers were definitely up Jennie's alley.

She closed her eyes and sighed, "Oh, yeah. Give me some hot guys missing their clothes!"

Maybe I should plan a weekend in Vegas for Jennie. I wasn't so sure Tampa could handle Jennie's fantasies. "You've got it. I am your slave."

"Finally. But seriously, tell me about the bitch. Get it off your chest. I know you've got all kinds of crazy suppressed inside."

I took another long sip of wine and adjusted the massager to work on my lower back. Sex with Jake last night had been fantastic and sleeping on the porch listening to the rain had essentially been a fantasy come true, but my back was arguing with me a bit more than usual.

"I don't know, I barely met her. I just got the impression she was two different people. She wears this mask of sweetness and fragility, but I know that isn't who she is."

"Why?"

"Sweet and fragile people don't hold their own with Greg. He eats them for breakfast or ignores them like they don't exist. He and Ashley can't stand each other. I watched them fight, her mask is only skin deep."

I wanted to tell Jennie why Greg hated Ashley, but it didn't feel right. I wasn't sure if it was where we were, or the timing, or what... but I held back that conversation. Maybe I just needed more time to digest it.

"If she pisses off Greg that much it could be fun to watch them at a party one day."

Did Jennie have a death wish? I shot her an evil glare and she held up her hands. "Sorry. Bad idea..."

Jennie absolutely hated having her feet touched. She winced and jerked throughout the entire pedicure. "Seriously, you are the strangest person. Why do you get pedicures?" I asked her.

She shrugged. "I like everything else. And when I'm done I have pretty feet! Besides, you're one to talk."

"Me?" I scoffed. I knew exactly what she was

talking about, but I was pleading ignorance.

"You swore you'd never do it again. *Swore*. And by swore I mean you cursed like a sailor and called me the worst best friend in all of eternity. And yet here you are..."

"What?" I asked innocently.

"I can't believe you're doing it." She shook her head and looked me up and down.

She could look all she wanted because I was doing it. I'd made my decision. "I'm only getting the bikini done this time." I could handle it. Last time, many, *many* years ago, Jennie had convinced me to get a Brazilian bikini wax. She loved them and got them all the time. She raved, went on and on about the virtues and how it really didn't hurt that much.

"Who was I dating then? Is it bad I can't even remember his name?"

"Brandon."

"Ohhhh..... yeah. I remember him now. The guy who liked wind surfing in the bay. He was crazy."

Brandon had been handsome enough. He had that blondish—I spend all my spare time outside—tan and rugged good looks. He was fun—that was why I'd dated him: he took me on one wild adventure after another. And he'd had a thing for my lady parts. He raved about them and thought they were gorgeous. I thought his enthusiasm was a bit weird. But we were going on a week-long trip to the beach, and Jennie convinced me I should give Brandon an eyeful.

Saying I swore like a pirate was probably being nice.

It had been hell. Why anyone intentionally did that to themselves baffled me. Every time I looked at Jennie in a bikini I couldn't stop thinking about that experience. Why did it seem so horrendous to me and barely phase her?

Maybe her vagina was made of stainless steel.

Jennie giggled then winced, yanking her foot away from the woman performing the pedicure. "Sorry... again..." The woman just shook her head and took Jennie's foot back.

"We're spending two weeks in bathing suits; I'm just getting a little bikini wax. It will be fine."

Luckily Jennie let it go. We were quiet for a little while and it was nice getting pampered. But Jennie was Jennie, and she couldn't keep quiet for too long. It just wasn't in her nature. "No second thoughts? I don't have to worry about a runaway bride or anything, right?"

I rolled my eyes. "God, no. The only thing driving me crazy is the whole long, drawn out process. Let's just get me hitched already."

"You're not nervous?"

"Not about Jake," I said quietly.

"What *are* you nervous about?"

"Life," I confessed. "I just want him to have the life he deserves."

Jennie leaned back over and made eyes at me. "Awww, you two are so cute. You've got the lovey dovey filters on."

I wrinkled my nose up at her. I didn't like the idea that my feelings for Jake were fake or altered.

"You're telling me you wouldn't do whatever it took to make Andrew happy?"

Jennie's eyebrows shot up. "Touché."

"I know Jake can take care of himself, but I don't want him to have to. Does that make sense?"

Jennie smiled at me. "Absolutely. You love him, he's your man. You'll walk through fire, climb mountains, and fend off hoards of zombies for his happiness, because his happiness is your happiness. His heart is your heart."

"Fuck," I swore under my breath. "Yeah, that." My chest actually ached a little thinking about it.

"That's why Greg calls you The Annihilator."

"He says what now?" I blurted out as I sat straight up in my chair. She had to be kidding. I mean, obviously Greg loved giving people nicknames, he and I together were a dangerous combination, but he'd given *me* a nickname... and I didn't even know about it?

"He calls you 'The Annihilator'," she said leaning back in her chair and closing her eyes, "because it's who you are. You destroy anything that gets in your path, and you're even worse when it comes to Jake. You two are adorably protective of each other. It's not a bad thing."

The thing was, I kind of loved that Greg had a nickname for me. I loved even more that it felt right. I desperately wanted to make Jake happy. Anything that got in the way of that... well, I was prepared to go to great lengths to eliminate it. I remembered Greg's words from lunch and realized just how seriously he meant them. *Heaven help anyone who gets between you and Jake.*

***

Thursday morning Jake and I loaded into the Orange Beast, Jake's refurbished orange Ford Bronco, for the drive south to my parent's house. The weather was perfect. The cold front had cooled everything off for the customary twenty-four hours and it was warming up nicely.

"Cassandra, Tim, and the boys are already there. June is flying in tonight because she couldn't get out of her morning class. And Tom is flying in late Friday. Greg is getting him from the airport and driving him down Saturday morning." I tucked the schedule back into my bag and leaned back in the seat, letting the air whip around me.

"Sounds like everything is covered, darlin'. You should start relaxing."

All I could do was laugh at his suggestion. There would be no relaxing until Sunday morning. Well... maybe there'd be *some* relaxing late Saturday night, after the wedding...

I looked over at Jake. He was grinning from ear to ear. There was a light stubble on his face that only made him more handsome, dark sunglasses, and a Ray's baseball cap covered his dark hair. He'd let it grow a little longer over the winter and the ends of it were curling. He looked more relaxed and carefree when his hair was longer. Younger. It was a beautiful day, cool in the shade but warm in the sun. He was wearing jeans and a long-sleeved t-shirt with the sleeves pushed up to his elbows.

"I have a present for you." I said it so softly I was afraid he didn't hear me at first.

But then he smiled. "I have a present for you, too."

"I want to give you mine before the wedding, if that's alright with you."

He nodded slowly, "Ok..."

I wasn't entirely sure what was coming over me, but I had a sudden intense urge to give him his present right then. He glanced over at me. "You want me to pull over, don't you?"

I bit my lip and nodded, "It's like Christmas. It's burning a hole in my pocket. How the hell did you make it a whole week in the Bahamas' with an *engagement ring* around your neck?"

He was thoroughly pleased with himself, the cocky bastard. His smile just about ripped his face in two. "I hear that patience is a virtue, and since I have so few, I thought I might practice that one."

"Jake, it is entirely possible you have more patience than any man alive. It's kind of infuriating."

Five minutes later he pulled off the interstate at possibly the most unromantic location possible: a barren parking lot in the middle of nowhere. But we were alone and I was absolutely giddy.

"Eve, you're vibrating. Take a deep breath."

"Oh shut it, Mr. Cool, Calm, and Collected. I'm excited." I pulled the black box out of my bag and turned it over in my hands a few times. I was more than excited, I was a little nervous. I didn't just want to be Jake's wife; I wanted to be his family. This gift was a little symbol of what family meant to me and I just hoped it helped him feel part of something bigger for a change.

I didn't look up at him. Instead, I kept my eyes on the box as I explained his gift. "Have you ever heard my family talk about our 'happy thoughts'?"

He shook his head slowly. "Not really. Maybe?"

"Do you know what a 'happy thought' is?" I asked.

"A thought that is happy?" he chuckled.

"It's from Peter Pan. Think of a happy thought and with a little magic, you can fly. In my family we have a tradition. We keep our happy thoughts around us. They are usually pictures or objects, but whatever we pick, they're something that makes us smile the instant we see it. A happy thought makes you feel like you can get through a bad day or gives you courage to keep going, but it is also a silent cheerleader. Every time you see your happy thought, you stop and take stock in what is going on around you, where you're headed, and how you're getting there. You can make your own happy thoughts, but sometimes we give them to each other as gifts, as well." I took a deep breath and held the box out to Jake. "This is my happy yhought, for you."

My heart was thudding inside my chest so hard it hurt. I wanted to cry and laugh and hug Jake until he felt as loved as he made me.

His green eyes were a little wider than normal as

he took the box from my hands. "The picture of me you keep on the visor in your car?"

"A happy thought," I replied with a smile.

"And the lock screen on your iPad... it's of you and your sisters at a game when you were kids."

"A happy thought, too. I keep one inside my Kindle case in my nightstand, under my keyboard at work, and the bottom of my underwear drawer."

"Your underwear drawer?" he asked, chuckling.

"Yep. When I'm late for work and freaking out, it's nice to have a picture of my dad showing me how to swing a bat to remind me to slow down. The world will still turn even if I'm a few minutes late."

Jake looked at the box in his hands for a long minute before saying anything else. He looked like he was just absorbing the idea. "Your necklace—the sunburst—that was my happy thought for a lot of years."

The necklace was around my neck and I pulled it out from under my sweater so Jake could see it. "And now, it's mine. Open yours."

He gave me a cocky half-grin and opened the box. Inside was a silver and black Tag Heuer watch. "My happy thought is a time piece?" he asked eyeing me carefully.

I grinned and reached out for the watch, taking it out of the box.

"Hey, get your grubby hands off my present, woman," he grumbled, batting away my hands and taking back the watch.

"Turn it over," I replied. My heart was going to

beat out of my chest if he didn't hurry up.

Jake released the clasp on the wrist band and flipped the watch over so that it was resting in the palm of his hand. A slow grin pulled up on the corners of his lips. "I love you so much it hurts. Thank you."

"You like it?"

He didn't say anything, just stared at the watch in his hands, running his thumb back and forth across the sunburst I'd had engraved on the back. It took me five jewelers to find someone who would do it. I never thought getting something engraved would be so hard, but it was. Inside of the sunburst there was an inscription: *Follow the sun, it will always lead you back to me.*

He slowly strapped the watch onto his wrist, then looked at the way it sat on his arm. He still didn't say anything as he reached out for the necklace around my neck, holding it in the palm of his hand and fighting a sea of emotions. He finally looked up, locking eyes with me. It took my breath away. His eyes were a little wild; the green was almost mixed with a shade of blue. It was like a storm. A beautiful, perfect storm. "Thank you," he said quietly. "It's perfect."

Chapter 12
-Jake-

There are three things I have indelibly etched into my brain from our wedding day. One was seeing Eve in the window of her parent's bedroom. The second was hearing her accidentally change our wedding vows. And the third was watching her come apart beneath me for the very first time as my wife.

I'd never been so overwhelmed. If it was anything like being a celebrity, then I never wanted to be famous.

There was always someone who wanted to talk to me (most I'd never met before) and there was always someone who needed something. Then there were the pictures. My face hurt from smiling so damn much.

Greg, Tom, and I were standing on the back porch trying to get a few minutes alone. It was good to see my uncle and to be together with the two men I considered my family.

Tom was shorter than me, but he was scary as hell. He was one of those guys who exuded power. You could feel it before he moved or spoke, it just surrounded him. And then, when he did finally speak, it confirmed everything your senses were telling you.

You didn't fuck with Tom.

He fidgeted while he stood next to Greg, pulling at his collar and constantly readjusting his cuffs. He was not a suit and tie kind of guy. His graying hair was cut very short, his skin was weathered, and his brown eyes were the kind that cut through everything.

I loved working for him. He was a no-nonsense kind of guy which was a huge part of his success. There was never any question where you stood with Tom.

"Should I sit you down and give you a talk about what's going to happen tonight?" Greg had such a serious expression on his face I actually second guessed whether he was joking or not. Maybe there was something else planned for our wedding night I didn't know about yet?

He and Tom traded "a look" and then both looked back at me expectantly.

"What?" I finally asked.

"Well you see," Greg started. He was so serious I didn't see it coming. "She's going to have a lot of expectations. It is a big night in the life of a woman and it is your responsibility to take care of her." Tom was nodding along and looking very concerned. "You're gonna want to hump her like a rabbit, but you've got to stop yourself."

Asshole. Only Greg could pull off shit like that with such a serious face. "Fuck off."

Greg and Tom both laughed at me. They were both assholes. Tom put his hand on my arm. "Seriously son, have you two talked about protection?"

I rolled my eyes. "I think we might have it covered." Truth was I wouldn't be devastated if we got pregnant. Having a kid with Eve would never be an accident.

"Do you have any questions?" Tom was almost as bad as Greg, but he was having trouble covering his smile.

I just shook my head. There was no stopping them until they got it all out of their systems. Maybe it was time for a whiskey.

"You two didn't do something stupid like abstain all week so your wedding night would be more 'special', did you?" Greg said it with a high-pitched voice.

Now I *knew* I needed a whiskey. I flagged down a waiter I saw flying by us with a tray of drinks. "Whiskey, *please.*"

"Bring the bottle," Tom said.

"Well did you?" Greg asked, looking pointedly at me. It was beyond me why he cared how much sex Eve and I were having.

"Do you know Eve at all, moron?" I shook my

head and adjusted my tux.

Tom laughed, "I like her. She's got spunk."

The truth was, nothing was different. We'd tried damn hard to make sure we were as normal as possible. We'd even slept in the same bed last night. I was supposed to leave before she woke up... but I didn't. I was pretty sure she was going to make me pay for that one.

But it was so worth it. I was awake before my alarm went off and I had one thing on my mind. My bride. She woke up to my tongue and my fingers teasing her into orgasm. I was almost positive she was asleep until just before it happened, because all of a sudden her fingers were in my hair as she tilted her hips against my lips. She was gasping and coming. It was perfect.

And then she yelled at me.

A lot.

Only Eve would get mad at a wake-up call like that. I grabbed my stuff and ducked out of the door while she hid under the sheet. In my defense, I never looked at her face.

"Jakey-poo!" June was running from the house waving an envelope in the air. Her blonde hair was down in long waves and her yellow dress was floating around her as she ran.

I swore under my breath and jogged over to meet Eve's youngest sister.

"Give me that..." I said, grabbing it from her hands.

She scowled at me. "You two are so weird. It's

just a letter. My money is on a torrid secret she's never told you before. The guilt is killing her, so she's confessing before you make a huge mistake."

Oh my little, innocent Junebug. If she only knew what was inside that envelope. I pulled my matching envelope out of my tuxedo jacket and leaned in. "If you call a list of places we want to have sex on our honeymoon a 'last minute confession' go right ahead. But I'd prefer you stop waving these in the air. Please."

She scrunched up her face like I'd just handed her a bucket of vomit and took the letter, pressing it against her chest. "Gross."

Maybe. But it was damn hot and fucking fun. "Just deliver the letter, June. And this." I handed her a small giftwrapped box.

She stuck her tongue out at me and left. When I turned around, Tom was gone and Greg was wandering toward the reception tent with our bottle of whiskey.

Since our "quick" wedding had become a rather massive affair there was a pre-wedding party going on in the tent for all the guests being bussed in from hotels and the mainland.

I could catch-up with Greg and Tom later—I wanted to see what Eve sent me.

I glanced up at the window and saw her outline. She was there and I knew she was watching me, but I was almost positive she didn't know I could see her. She looked beautiful. There was a smile on her face and her dark hair was loose and wild the way I liked it. It always made me think she was ready for anything. I grinned and winked up at her just before I looked back down at the letter.

There was only one line and it was full of pure evil: *I hear patience is a virtue, you should practice.*

I resisted the urge to crumple the card in my fist as raw sexual frustration raced through my veins. Eve knew me far too well. If there was one way to drive me crazy and want her more than I already did, it was to dangle mystery sex in front of me.

When I glanced back up at the window I could see her much clearer than before. Sometimes I wasn't sure what I believed about life and death, but when I looked at Eve, I knew I believed in one thing.

I believed in angels.

It was the easiest way to explain how I felt about her. She showed me a life I didn't know I could have. She believed in me when I didn't believe in myself.

She helped save me from myself and that sounded an awful lot like an angel to me.

Chapter 13
~Eve~

June returned with my envelope from Jake. "You two are weird." She thrust the envelope and a box into my waiting hands and turned to leave.

"You're just jealous," I teased her back.

She turned at the doorway to stick her finger down her throat and fake a few gagging noises. "I'm surrounded by a bunch of love freaks!"

I didn't argue. I just tucked the letter into my bag to read later. The exchanging of cards wasn't really for me—it was for Jake. I knew the day was going to be overwhelming and I thought the letter would help serve as a distraction. Based on the grin I just saw through the window, I had succeeded.

Then I looked at the box in my hands. It was wrapped in thick cream paper with a blue bow on top. It wasn't large, just big enough to fit in the palm of my hand. It must have been gift-wrapped. I couldn't imagine Jake with his large hands folding the expensive paper so precisely. I set the envelope aside and pulled at the corners of my gift. Inside was a box with the distinctive blue of Tiffany's.

My heart was racing as I opened it, but it fell into my stomach and stopped beating altogether as I saw what was cradled inside. Sitting against the satin fabric was a gold necklace. Hanging from the chain, encrusted in diamonds, was a perfect golden sun. There was a small card tucked in beside it.

For special occasions and new happy thoughts. I love you.

I touched the necklace he'd given me last year. I was already wearing it, and had planned on wearing it down the aisle. It wasn't nearly as fancy or expensive as this new necklace, but it was perfect because Jake gave it to me. I sat and stared at my present for a few minutes. The contrast between the two was hitting me hard. The necklace around my neck was a tie to our past, but it was also a testament to our journey. The necklace in my hands was precious and beautiful, like our future.

With a deep breath and a lot of emotions I was trying desperately to wrangle, I pulled the delicate necklace out and walked over to the mirror.

I didn't take off my old necklace. Instead, I put the new one on and let them dangle around my neck side by side. Our past and our future. Our inner demons beside our outer façade. There was no telling where the next ten years were going to take us. Most of the time that idea thrilled me. It seemed so full of love and possibilities.

But sometimes it scared the crap out of me.

There was so much uncertainty. So many different ways our lives could unfold, and every day I was more connected to Jake.

Just as I tucked Jake's envelope and box into my bag for the hotel, Jennie and Cassandra drifted into the room wearing gowns nearly identical to June's. Jennie's blonde hair was swept up into a bun while Cassandra's dark hair was down in waves like June's.

"Everything seems to be going well. We should be on schedule for the wedding of the year!" Jennie grinned at me.

I was apparently silly to think our fast wedding would turn off most potential guests. Instead, the opposite happened. Everyone was thrilled to help pull off our wedding and determined to be there to see it happen. It was overwhelming and I was definitely nervous about having such a *big* day.

Honestly, it had turned into a circus. January was the height of the busy tourist season on the islands, so most of the hotels were already booked. My parents called in every favor they could manage and found most of the guests somewhere to stay, the rest were staying off-island in Fort Myers. We'd hired cars and vans to ferry guests to and from their respective hotels to the house. We lived on an island—there was no way we were ever going to park three-hundred cars.

Guests were arriving in shifts so my parents arranged a pre-party. I could hear the soft sounds of the DJ playing music in the reception tent. There were party games, cocktails, and food.

Not that I cared about any of it.

All I cared about was marrying Jake.

And while I was nervous about the fuss everyone was making, I wasn't the least bit worried about the monumental thing we were about to do. I knew without a doubt marrying Jake was right.

Cassandra flitted around to check my hair. "You're perfect, Evie."

I'd taken Jake at his word when he said he wanted to see me in a sexy white dress. "I hope Jake likes it."

She and Jennie traded smiles. "Sister dear, I'm not sure if you know this, but your groom would love you in just about anything. He's kind of got blinders on when it comes to you. I think he'd find you sexy in a garbage bag."

She had a point. It wasn't about the dress, though. Even I knew that. I wanted today to be perfect. Not for me, but for Jake. He said this wedding was for me, and it was, but it was also for him. There were very few nice, normal traditions in his life. Having a dream wedding was something I could give him. I wanted everything to go smoothly.

"Alright, we need to get you in that dress so we can start in on pictures."

It wasn't a hard dress to put on, but like everything else with this wedding, it was a process clouded with emotions.

As I wiggled into the backless dress with Cassandra on one side and Jennie on the other, I knew these memories were going to stay with me forever.

They stepped back and did that thing where they scrunched up their faces to stop the tears, but it didn't work. Cassandra broke first and I was gonna blame it on her mommy-hormones, but Jennie was right behind her.

"Guys, come on. This is supposed to be a happy day. You're starting to make me feel weird."

Jennie hugged me. "You're such an idiot sometimes. We are crying because we're so happy we can't keep it in."

Cassandra was nodding her head vehemently. "So happy."

That was when my mom walked in. She stopped dead in her tracks and clapped her hand over her mouth as she did the same face scrunchy thing.

"That's it!" I yelled. "All three of you, downstairs. I'll see you for pictures and nothing else. Send in June."

I heard her telltale snicker from the hallway. "Move along criers, move along." She waved them out of the room and shut the door. "I gotcha, no worries. Now, let's make sure you are picture perfect."

She and I went over my hair and makeup, double checked my dress and underwear, then she helped me into my flip flops. Yes, I said flip flops. I was getting married on the beach, it was either barefoot (which was my choice) or flip flops. I'd been talked into the shoes. Apparently it was "safer". Something about no one wanting an emergency on my wedding day.

I argued the point that I never wore shoes outside of work and I'd live if I stepped on something, but I was overruled.

"It's not too late to back out. I can smuggle you out the front."

"June, what the hell? This is my wedding day and all you've done is act like—" I stopped and looked my baby sister up and down. Her eyes were sad, her shoulders slumped, and her smile was obviously forced. "Did someone break your heart?"

She shifted uncomfortably and looked away. June obviously had something happen to her and was trying to hide it with all the wedding chaos going on around her.

"Not exactly. I was an idiot, ok? I shouldn't have been so stupid."

I definitely didn't like the sound of that. "Sit, tell me all about it."

She glared at me and crossed her arms. "I'm supposed to get you downstairs in five minutes for pictures."

"Then make it quick." I stared her down with my very best Big Sister eyes. "Sit."

She huffed, but sat down. "I'm telling you, I was stupid and I'll get over it."

"You don't have to give me all the details, just explain why you're hurting."

She shifted around and all I wanted to do was hug her, but I knew June better than that. She would stiffen up and push me away. She'd put her guard back up and it would be the end of everything. So I resisted my sisterly urge to love her and gave her space.

"I got involved with someone I knew wasn't available."

"Married?"

She shook her head, "Oh, god no. Nothing like that. Just, not available for a relationship or feelings or anything like that. We agreed to just keep things light, we saw each other as friends and we were experimenting with some fun on the side…"

She wouldn't meet my eyes and her cheeks flushed. "June, you're a beautiful twenty year old woman. I'm not going to judge your choices. You are old enough to know what you need."

She smiled a little and shrugged her shoulders. "Thanks. Bottom line, I knew better. I knew I liked him too much. Things got complicated and we had a huge fight before I left to come here."

Now that she'd poured out her heart, I tackle hugged her. I wrapped my arms around her and tucked her head against my shoulder. "Boys are stupid. I'm sorry you had to come to my wedding when your own heart was hurting."

June pulled away and wiped a stray tear from the corner of her eye. She hated crying as much as I did so I was surprised to see her so worked up. June must really like this guy. "Is there anything I can do?

Any advice I can give? As you may or may not know, I'm kind of experienced at complicated relationships." I was hoping the self-deprecation would help lighten things.

She looked around the room and shrugged. "Is it worth it?"

"Is *what* worth it?" I asked. This was a very important question and I didn't want to misunderstand her.

"Relationships. I have friends and family... do I really need a relationship?"

"A funny question to ask on my wedding day."

She smiled. "I'm cool like that. It's a trick question designed to make sure you're really ready to get hitched."

The truth in her statement made me want to hug her until her heart stopped hurting, but I knew all too well it wouldn't help. The only thing that helps heartaches like that is time.

"June, life is a crazy bitch. There is nothing fair or easy about it. If you find someone who makes you hopeful even when there's no hope, if he makes you want to be a better person, and if he is willing to give everything for your happiness, then yes. But anything less will just break your heart and bring you down. You need someone to weather the storm with, not be the storm. Life is going to get hard and when that happens, having someone at your side can make it easier to survive. So when you think you're falling in love, step back and ask yourself, is he someone who will help you survive, or someone you have to survive."

"I'm really happy you're getting married to Jake." She forced a smile onto her face, but I knew her words were genuine.

"Me too."

Chapter 14
-Jake-

Greg and I were playing darts on the back porch when Tom walked up. "Can I steal the groom for a few minutes?"

"As long as you get him drunk," Greg said with a shrug. "He's far too sober for what he's about to do."

Greg could fuck off. I never could understand why he was always so intent on getting me drunk. "We can talk in here," I replied, leading my uncle into the sitting room of Joe and Mara's house. Eve and her family were off doing pictures in the garden and I'd been told to stay away.

The sitting room had tall windows on two sides overlooking the beach. There were two simple blue couches facing each other and two white arm chairs with a dark wood coffee table in the middle. China and antiques dotted the furniture and walls and heavy blue curtains hung around the windows.

I took a seat on the couch facing the door and Tom took the chair beside me. He leaned forward over his knees and clasped his hands together. "I just wanted to have a few minutes alone with you. I haven't seen in you months, it's been weird."

Tom was always busy. It wasn't as if I saw him all the time when I worked for him, but now I *never* saw him. "I miss you, too. But I don't miss the work and I don't miss the desert." If I set foot in the Middle East ever again, it would be too soon. In fact, I didn't think I ever wanted to visit another desert. I hoped that was ok with Eve.

"I don't blame you. It was never your thing. In my defense, I tried to get you to leave for years."

"That you did."

I got the feeling Tom was working up to something. He wasn't the most expressive man I'd ever met, he never minced words, but he typically got his point across.

"I have something I want to say—something I should have said a long time ago..." he paused, looking everywhere but at me before finally spitting it out. "I should have gotten you out of that house a lot sooner. I'm sorry."

I never wanted or expected an apology like that from my uncle, so his words knocked me on my ass. "Don't be ridiculous, you have nothing to apologize for."

He looked right into my eyes. "I don't want to debate this, son. This isn't a heart-to-heart conversation. This is me telling you I'm sorry. I should have gotten you out of there sooner. Period. And that's the beginning and end of this conversation."

He stared me down, daring me to say another word, but I knew better than that. Tom said what he needed to say, and that was final. "Ok."

He nodded once and took a deep breath. "Good. You're a good kid and I've never wanted anything but the best for you. I'm very proud of you and the work you've done and I can't wait to see what you and Eve do with your lives."

I kind of strangely liked it when Tom called me "son". I knew it was as much a general comment on my age as an actual endearment, but considering I'd disowned my real father and thought of Tom as my next best alternative, it felt good to hear.

"Thank you, sir."

"So don't fuck it up." He said it so bluntly.

"Trust me, I won't," I replied slowly. I really wasn't sure where Tom was going with this.

He cracked his neck and rubbed his palms together before replying. "Look, Greg told me what's going on with Ashley. You need to put her on the next plane to Timbuktu, not sit in meetings talking to her."

This was about Ashley? Well at least it was something manageable. "We are all adults. I can handle her just fine, sir."

Tom rolled his eyes. "I'm not questioning your ability to handle her, Jake. I'm asking why you are bothering with it." He sighed and ran his free hand through his short hair, swearing under his breath. "Why is she here? Appearing out of nowhere with no warning? Pushing a business deal? Nothing but trouble will come out of having her in Tampa."

It was one thing to listen to Greg complain about Ashley, but it was quite another to hear it from Tom. My uncle didn't sit around talking about the weather. If he was bringing it up it was because he was genuinely concerned.

And if Tom was genuinely concerned then I needed to stop and really listen to what he had to say, whether I liked it or not.

And I really didn't like it.

He sighed, looking like saying this was about as much fun for him as it was for me. "I think you're giving her a free pass now because you feel bad for her. But she's not you, Jake. She's more damaged than you ever were. Most of us can't get knocked down and get right back up. *But you can.* No matter how many times you got knocked down, you *always* got back up. For you, there is, and always will be, a solution. It is who you are and nothing, not even your dad, could change that. But Ashley isn't like you. She's different. And her past has ruined her. Having her near you is toxic, but having her around your new life—and the woman who is about to become your wife—is simply not worth it."

Tom was absolutely right about one thing: Ashley was more fucked up than I was. But I found it hard to write her (or anyone else) off as a lost cause. I always sympathized with her because, like me, her past wasn't her choice. We were both trying to find a way to survive a life we didn't ask to live. But was having her in Tampa toxic? I couldn't imagine anything coming between me and Eve, certainly not a few days of Ashley.

"And I should never trust a redhead." I joked because I really needed a moment to cover my thoughts.

Tom barked out a laugh, slapping his hand against his thigh. "You *do* listen to me. Bottom line, I want you and Eve to have the best shot, and that means overstepping my bounds from time to time to tell you what I think is best for you, son."

Maybe I was giving Ashley a free pass because I wanted to help, but that was all it was, or ever would be. It was nice of Tom to worry about us, but there was nothing to worry about. Eve and I were fine, and Ashley was a non-factor. "I'm glad you're here today. Thank you for coming."

"I wouldn't have missed it for the world." It was probably the closest Tom and I would ever come to saying something sentimental.

The door to the sitting room suddenly opened and Greg popped his head in, "Hey buttercup! You guys done in here yet?"

"You feeling lonely, sweetheart?" I teased him back.

Greg stepped all the way inside, his whiskey glass permanently attached to his hand. "Fuck yeah. It isn't fair when you two play without me on the playground."

"I'm sorry. Do you need your dolly?"

Greg snorted and took a swig of his drink. "Naw, but you might. It's time, buttercup. Let's go get you hitched."

Chapter 15
~Eve~

"You get twenty minutes. Not a minute longer." I glared at my mother. She was being impossible.

"Thirty."

"No. You said *this* would take thirty minutes and I've been smiling for over an hour. There are only so many pictures that can be taken in one day and I'm already at my limit!"

"You haven't even taken pictures with Jake yet!"

"Which is why you get twenty more minutes after the ceremony."

She crossed her arms and looked me up and down. She was trying to figure out how serious I was being. "Fine."

"I'm serious mother, I'm walking at exactly twenty minutes. This is my wedding day and I am not going to miss out on enjoying it because you want a picture of my hair from fifteen different angles!"

She stopped and got all misty eyed on me again. She was going to be the death of me. Every single time someone said "wedding day" or "bride" or even "Eve", she turned into a tear factory.

Jennie saw my frustration and stepped in, "Come on, Mara, let's make sure the flowers are ready."

My mother nodded and allowed Jennie to lead her away. June had disappeared sometime after the first round of pictures so it was just Cassandra and me. "It's almost over and you and your groom can ride off *alone* into the sunset." She smiled and adjusted my hair again.

"He tricked me this morning, you know. He didn't leave when he was supposed to."

Cassandra faked a look of shock. "Heaven's no! Don't tell me the man hopelessly in love with you was still in your bed this morning. For shame!"

I chuckled. "Even worse. He woke me up with his mouth."

At first my sister shrugged and then paused. She arched her eyebrow and looked me up and down. "Really? What a fantastic wedding present."

"It really was. But I'm not letting him know that for a while."

"Evil."

I shrugged. Teasing Jake was one of my joys in life.

Dad came around the corner. He was trying to smile, but he was failing miserably. "Daughter! Are you ready for this?"

"I am." I slid my hand into the crook of his arm while my sister took the other.

He looked from me to Cassandra and back again. "I'm about to have two married daughters. It's hard to believe."

I rested my cheek against his strong shoulder as we walked slowly toward our waiting guests.

"You act like it's a bad thing, Dad," Cassandra laughed. We always gave him a hard time because if he had his way, we'd still be eight and living at home.

"No, you both picked fine men. I'm proud of both of you and the lives you're building. It's just... I don't like change."

I lifted my head up. "Now see, if you all had let me get married in Vegas instead, I could have spared Dad all this drama!"

He shook his head and put his arm over my shoulder. "Oh no, you can't rob me of my opportunity to walk you down the aisle."

My mom rushed toward us with bouquets in each hand and June right behind her. "Everything is ready. You say the word and we'll get started."

I smiled at my family. We were only missing Jake. "I'm ready."

It was the middle of January so the weather was chilly and the blue skies were completely clear. An arch covered in wild flowers stood at one end, with a semicircle of white chairs around it. There was an aisle of sand carefully raked for the procession.

My dad wasn't talking, I knew he was too choked up. He'd rather just keep things quiet, besides there was no need for words between us. I, on the other hand, was quite ready to get this over.

I smiled, looking back and forth, taking a moment to say hello, until my eyes fell on Jake.

So many guests standing had hidden him from me until we were halfway down the aisle.

It didn't matter how many times I'd spied on him throughout the day, seeing Jake this close took my breath away. I could see the creases around his eyes from smiling, and his dimple.

I was deliriously happy and so was he. In a few minutes we were going to *officially* be married. No more *feeling* like we were already married and no more promises or expectations. This was it.

Time seemed to slip away from me, moving at breakneck speed one moment and crawling the next. My heart was racing and everything seemed surreal, like I was floating, not walking.

Greg was standing beside Jake with an equally silly grin on his face, and beside Greg was Tom, who was as choked up as my dad.

My father stopped me at the end of the aisle, physically holding me back from joining Jake at the altar. "Not yet daughter," he winked.

I nodded, catching his eye, but completely incapable of saying anything.

"Who gives this woman to this man?"

My father smiled and I bet he could guess what was going through my head: *no one was giving me to this man but me.* "Her mother and I do." Then he took a deep, deep breath, turned to me and kissed me on my cheek. "I love you daughter. Always and forever."

I kissed him back on his other cheek and we hugged as if this simple act of marriage were somehow tearing me away from my family and sending me to the other side of the world, never to be seen again.

Then I turned to Jake—who was smiling and waiting patiently—and my heart took off in a whole new direction.

Jake looked damn sexy in his tux. Somehow he looked taller than normal, stronger, and he smelled amazing. It made me lightheaded and giggly like we'd just met. It was ridiculous.

I put my hands inside Jake's and took a deep breath, but I couldn't wipe the enormous grin off my face. I thought brides were supposed to cry, but that was the last thing on my mind. Sure I was completely overwhelmed standing in front of three hundred people with the man I loved, but I was so happy I couldn't stop smiling.

Jake's smile was just as big as mine, we probably looked crazy. I never once looked at the preacher, and I barely registered the first few rows of people. All I saw was Jake and his enormous, handsome smile. I was lost inside his green eyes and he was just as lost inside mine.

As the preacher spoke the vows, Jake nodded and squeezed my hand.

Then he repeated the words to me. Jake was so sincere and passionate about his vows, there was an unshakable truth to his words.

"I, Jake Spencer, take you, Eve Maria Daniels, to be my *wife*." He smiled, then suddenly took my hand and pressed it to his heart the way he sometimes did when he was telling me how much he loved me. The feel of his heart beating so strong and steady beneath my palm, with his larger, rough hand holding it in place was probably the most intimate thing I'd ever felt then or since. "I promise to be true to you in good times and in bad." He paused and pressed my hand against his chest harder, and added, "I promise."

I nodded, my eyes locked onto his. His promise had somehow traveled the space between us, threading itself under my skin and nestling around my heart like Jake was personally protecting it.

"... in sickness and in health. I will love and honor you all the days of my life."

The crowd around us was so quiet I could feel them. And as I started my vows I heard random sniffling from the audience. Jake hadn't just taken my breath away, he'd taken everyone's.

"I, Eve Maria Daniels, take you, Jake Spencer Junior, to be my husband. I promise to be true to you in good times and in bad, in sickness and in health. I will *love*," I breathed the word. It just wasn't strong enough for how I was feeling. "... and *honor you forever*."

Jake smiled at my little variation on the end of my vows. But it was true. I wouldn't just love Jake all the days of my life or his.

I would never stop loving Jake.

Seconds later, the preacher was asking us for the rings. I slid Jake's ring on and whispered, "All mine now... last chance to run."

He shook his head and leaned in closer, "Not on your life. You are stuck with me."

Then he pulled out my ring and slid it onto my finger. But before I could admire how it looked to wear his symbol of marriage, Jake pulled my hand to his lips and placed a slow, careful kiss on my ring. "Forever."

The preacher was talking, but I didn't hear him, not until he said, "You may kiss the bride," and Jake swept me up into his arms with my feet off the ground with my hands around his face, and we kissed.

A long, long kiss. My lips pressed firmly against his.

This time I finally heard something other than Jake. I heard the roaring crowd around us as they cheered on our kiss. It made Jake chuckle, it sent vibrations up through my body. Suddenly I wanted the crowd to disappear so Jake and I could be alone.

But instead he set me down and shook his head, "Later Mrs. Spencer. We have a party to attend first."

I shrugged my shoulders and turned, my hand tucked into my husband's elbow as the preacher announced, "May I present Mr. and Mrs. Jake Spencer," to our friends and family.

We walked down the aisle on a cloud and ran (yes, ran) to the guest house for a moment of privacy.

***

The microphone was the most popular thing at our reception. Everyone wanted a crack at it. Some told silly stories, others simply wanted to wish us the best. My sisters both made me cry. They made really touching speeches about growing up together and how perfectly Jake fit into our family.

From that point on I laughed and cried until I was completely exhausted. Jake's arm was around my waist at all times and his other hand was wrapped around mine in his lap. The only time it was free was for drinking champagne. Which, I might add, was refreshing and delicious.

During Greg's speech, which was admittedly enhanced by a good amount of whiskey, my nephew Teddy wiggled his way over to us and settled himself in Jake's lap. Those two together—it did things to me. Teddy adored his new uncle. They had an instant and special bond, the kind that can't be explained any more than my bond with Jake. The little boy was tired and curled up in Jake's lap like it was the most comfortable place in the world. And Jake... he was grinning like a fool in love (with someone other than me) and gently rubbing Teddy's back. He was instinctively rocking back and forth just a little.

When he noticed me watching him, he smiled and winked, squeezing my hand before turning back to listen to Greg's blubbering.

"... I just, can't tell you how proud of you I am, man. Really and truly. After all these years to finally see this woman I've heard all about. Eve is everything you said she was, and, well fuck—*sorry!*— I'm just so happy for you both."

Greg came around and hugged Jake so he wouldn't have to disturb Teddy who was nearly asleep. Then he hugged me (I don't think he was sober enough to realize how hard he was hugging me) and whispered in my ear, "Welcome to the family, Evie. I hope to have a little nephew like Teddy very soon."

It wasn't the first time something like that had been said. It seemed to be a wedding tradition. Once the ring was on your finger it was time to talk babies.

The thing was—I wasn't ready. Jake and I had only been back together a few months. Sure we had four years together, but that was a lifetime ago. We were different people with different lives back then. I wanted time with him, all to myself. Kids changed everything, I knew that.

Looking at how Jake was blissfully snuggling our nephew though, I knew it was something we were going to have to talk about sooner than later. We'd successfully avoided it up until this point, along with a lot of other things. It was a silent pact between us to avoid subjects like that until after the wedding. Maybe it was stupid. We were two intelligent, level-headed people. Surely we could discuss things as important as our future. But I was secretly terrified those topics would be grounds for fighting and disagreement. I desperately wanted to avoid disagreement at all costs. I just wanted to be happy with Jake for a little while longer.

So, I pretended no one had mentioned kids, and when I looked at Jake holding Teddy, all I saw was a man madly in love with his adorable nephew.

Between the champagne and the emotions, I was jonesing for some emotional relief. So the moment Tim whisked Teddy away, I whisked Jake away. It was no small task to disappear from your own wedding, but thankfully it was dark, so with a little maneuvering I was able to sneak us out the side of the tent and down the walkway to my mother's rose garden.

"Where are we going, darlin'?" Jake was laughing.

"I need you," I replied with my own giggle of mischief.

If there was one thing that would relax me, it was Jake. The house was off-limits, so we couldn't go there. The guest houses were being used for entertaining and the luxury portable bathrooms were set up right beside them. It was almost as busy there as it was inside the reception tent.

So I was taking Jake to the only place I could think of where we might actually be able to find a few moments of peace.

"You seriously can't wait another hour? We'll be in a limo, we could do it there..."

"Too cliché!" I yelled over my shoulder. And no, I seriously couldn't wait an hour.

"We have a gorgeous hotel room waiting for us,

babe. I can lay you out and do you right. Any which way you want, your choice!"

"No, I need you *now*." I repeated. We were in the garden now. It was small and surrounded on three sides by a hedge. There were brick pavers with a giant water fountain in the middle, and three stone benches around it. The rose bushes were in pots artfully arranged around the garden.

I pulled Jake around to the back side of the fountain where we would be hidden even if someone else followed us down here. "Sit," I commanded.

But he didn't. No, instead he pulled me into his arms and pressed my head to his wide chest. "Talk to me. What's going on?"

I burrowed in a little closer. "Emotional overload. Too many people saying too many things."

He squeezed me to him, it felt so nice. Being inside Jake's arms was the most relaxing place in the world.

"I haven't even gotten a chance to give my speech yet," he said as he kissed the top of my head.

I sighed, "I don't think I can take any more speeches tonight."

Jake laughed, "Babe, they're just happy for us. Let them have their chance to tell us. Weddings are only one night. We have a lot of years ahead of us, you may regret not having these memories to fall back on when times get tough."

"Can't we avoid tough times for the rest of our lives?" I knew it was a stupid question. But really, reality had no place existing on my wedding day.

He shook his head slowly, tilting my chin up so he could look into my eyes, "Nope. I will try my damnedest to keep them as far away from us as I can, but it will happen. And I want you to have memories like this—your family and friends telling you how much they love you."

"They're *our* family and friends now, Jake. Not just mine."

Jake's jaw stiffened and a look flashed through his eyes. He took my face in his hands and kissed me. No more time for chaste kisses. His tongue wove deep into my mouth as he pulled my body firmly against his. Suddenly Jake didn't seem so opposed to my desperate plea for relief.

I repeated my earlier command to sit, and this time he did.

I sat on his lap facing him, with my legs wrapped around his waist. I had to gather up a lot of white skirt to get there, and Jake helped, arranging my skirt around us like a blanket as I settled against him.

He groaned and I felt him begin to harden. "What are you doing to me, Eve?"

"What you and I do." By now he was nice and firm inside his tuxedo pants. "Why, Mr. Spencer, I do believe you are attracted to your bride."

He seductively ran his nose up my throat and nuzzled behind my ear where I loved it so much. I was growing wetter by the second and I could feel the heat building between my legs. I was so desperate for relief and it wouldn't take much.

He kissed the hollow of my neck and ran his hands

up and down the bare back of my dress. "Babe, can I just say... when I told you to wear a sexy white dress... well, I had no idea. You look amazing. It's been hard to keep my hands off you all night."

"Good," I whispered in his ear.

He squeezed me tighter and pulled my body down on his hard cock. It made me flutter deep inside where I wanted to feel him.

"This is pushing things, even for us, darlin'." He said it pointedly and looking straight in my eyes. I think he was asking me what was really going on without actually saying the words. He wanted me to talk to him, but I couldn't bring myself to say the things swirling inside my head.

"We'll be quick," I whispered, my hands digging down beneath my skirt to his pants.

"Eve! Jake!"

The sound of Jennie's voice froze both of us where we were. I swallowed, knowing my bid for relief was being abandoned. Even if Jennie didn't see us over here, there was no way Jake was going to finish what I started.

"Oh, for the love of all!" she exclaimed, throwing her hands in the air the minute she found us. "You two are seriously humping in the garden during your own wedding reception?"

I smiled sheepishly and slid my hands back out of Jake's lap so I could shrug my shoulders. "There should be no doubts that Jake and I are hot for each other."

Jennie put her hands on her hips and faked a

scowl. "Eve, no one on earth doubts that. Now, pull yourselves together and get back inside that tent. If we don't have cake soon there's going to be a riot."

Five minutes later we posed for pictures around an enormous white cake. "You smear this on my face and sex is off the table tonight," I warned him under my breath.

He wrapped his large hand around mine as I put the edge of the silver knife against the smooth white frosting. He whispered in my ear, "I can think of much better places to put this cake, darlin'."

My whole body quivered and I bit my lip as I looked back at my new husband, "Promise?"

He nodded slowly, his green eyes locked onto mine. "I never joke around when it comes to eating cake."

"Mom!" I yelled, turning over my other shoulder. I knew she was standing right on the edge of the crowd.

"What do you need Eve? Is the knife ok?"

"Yes, the knife is ok. I need two slices of the chocolate cake boxed up for us to take to the hotel."

"Taken care of!" she scoffed with a wave of her hand and immediately flagged down a waiter who scurried off to get us a box.

"Ready, Mr. Spencer?"

"Indeed, Mrs. Spencer." He pushed the knife through the cake, slicing out a piece for each of us. We carefully fed each other, all while giggling mischievously. Wedding day sex was getting more and more exciting.

Chapter 16
-Jake-

I'd had to fend off my new wife all night. My dirty girl tried to seduce me in the garden and then she tried to bribe me into leaving the wedding early. She was ridiculous. *It was awesome.*

But I had plans for her.

I wanted her to have the perfect wedding and then I wanted her to have the perfect wedding *night*. We agreed to leave the past in the past and most of the time I was content with our agreement.

But sometimes I couldn't. I think I would always feel a little bit of a burden to make my disappearance up to her. I would always carry that guilt around with me. So there was no way I was getting talked out of the perfect wedding for Eve and there was absolutely no way she was ruining my plans for our first time together as husband and wife.

"Do you know this is a fantasy of mine?" I asked.

Eve was standing across from me as I closed the door to the honeymoon suite.

"The wedding night? Claiming your bride and making her yours?"

I shook my head. "Nope. Too old fashioned. I like to think a little more progressively."

She arched her eyebrow and pursed her lips.

Hot.

"Ok," I relented. "So I'm stretching the truth a little."

She smiled wickedly and it was all I could do to stop myself from shredding her wedding dress right then and there. "What's your fantasy, Jake?"

I shivered every time she said my name. "The white dress."

Her breathing hitched and her eyes narrowed. "*Oh...*"

It was my turn to smile. She had no idea what she was in for. "Yeah, *oh*. It only happens once. I only get to defile you in that sexy, perfect, *white* dress once. And I'm going to enjoy every second."

She licked her lips and took a step back toward the bed.

"Oh no you don't, Mrs. Spencer. Stay right where you are."

She froze mid-step, her chest was rising and falling and her eyes were following me, but that was it. She was mine.

I kissed every inch of her exposed skin as I took my time. Kissing down her back was my favorite part. The way she responded to my touch, gasping and begging for more... I had to have my way with her.

Starting with that dress.

I ran my hand down her bare back. "Backless but strangely appropriate. Sexy and sensual yet not risqué in the slightest. This dress is perfect, Eve. It's just like you—the perfect combination."

She smiled softly as she watched me over her shoulder. Her hair fell around her face and down her back. "You asked for a sexy white dress, I delivered."

She had no idea. "It is a very good look on you, darlin'. You should look into getting more."

She shivered under my touch. "With a reaction like that, how could I not?"

I swallowed as I tried to keep myself together.

Then I pushed the dress down her arms, finding exactly what I hoped: no bra. "You are my dream and destruction all mixed into one," I groaned.

But then I ran my fingers inside her dress, wiggling the delicate lace fabric down her hips and found her underwear. "You have *not* been wearing these all night..." I whispered. The back was little more than a white satin string held together by gold rings.

"Of course I have," she smiled, arching her back. "Why do you think I kept trying to sneak off with you. It would have been so easy to have some quick, naughty fun at our wedding."

It hurt. It physically hurt to know I missed out on seeing that underwear earlier in the night. I probably would have stuck to my plan, but at least I would have had the visual. Patience wasn't all it was cracked up to be.

"Those are staying on. For now anyway." I pushed the dress down to the floor and held her hand while she stepped out. "Don't move."

I wanted to take a moment and appreciate everything that was my new wife. Only one light was on in the room and it bathed everything in the room in a soft yellow glow that reflected off her skin. She looked flawless. Her dark hair curled around her shoulders, falling just above her peaked and perfect nipples. She was toned and firm, but soft and supple in all the right places. I knew exactly what Eve looked like, and yet every time I saw her naked body it was a surprise.

"You have far too many clothes on," she chastised.

I grinned from ear to ear as I tugged at the tie around my neck. "Let me fix that."

"Can I, or is that against the wedding night rules?"

She was teasing me, of course. I stepped toward her, suddenly feeling oddly nervous. "Don't let me stop you."

Eve pushed back my jacket, letting it fall to the floor, then moved to the top button of my shirt. "This is my favorite part. Other people get to talk to you, have meetings with you, work with you, but I'm the only one who gets to take off your clothes and see what's hidden underneath."

I grabbed her hand, stopping her mid button, wrapped my arm around her waist and kissed her hard on the mouth.

She was the only one who *ever* saw what was hidden underneath.

When I pulled back from the kiss her eyes were softer than usual. She was breathless. "I love you, husband," she whispered as she stroked her hand across my cheek.

I didn't think Eve would ever understand how much I loved her, but I was going to try every day for the rest of my life to show her, starting with a wedding night she would never forget.

I swept her up into my arms and took her to bed. It was huge and soft. Eve sank into the mattress as soon as I laid her down beneath me. We didn't say much after that. I think we were both too overwhelmed for words. Instead we communicated through sounds and hands. I made love to her slowly and her orgasm came on just as slowly. It built and built until she was sweating and shaking around me. She was so breathless she could barely say my name as we came together for the first time as husband and wife.

"I'm exhausted," she sighed five minutes later. Neither one of us had moved.

"That was a pretty intense workout. We should shower and eat a snack. You know," I grinned. "Refuel for round two."

Only her eyes moved. "Round two?"

"Cake."

Her eyes lit up and a slow grin pulled at the corners of her lips. "Start the shower. I'll be there in a minute."

I helped her shower. Eve really was exhausted, but by the time I had her soaped up she was laughing and joking again. "Do you think Greg will remember our wedding?"

I turned off the shower and opened the glass door. "Honestly? I'm not sure. He wasn't himself today."

We dried off and climbed back into bed with our leftovers. I placed the cake in the middle of the bed as a prize. "Food, then fun."

"As if I would have it any other way." Eve was already shoving food in her mouth. "Did you have a good day?"

I stopped mid chew. "Of course! Did you?" Maybe I'd missed out on some inside drama before the wedding?

"I did," she said slowly, setting her food down. "It was a beautiful day. I just wanted to make sure you had a good day too."

"I married you. It was the perfect day." This woman had a way of making me feel more things that I knew what to do with.

She nodded and picked her food back up, finishing off a sampling of a dozen different things they'd served at our reception. It was an insane amount of food. "Cake?"

"Yes, please..."

But the real question was *how* to eat it. I wanted to eat it all off of her in tiny little bites. But then again, having her return the favor could be a lot of fun, too.

Turns out I didn't need to worry. There was more

cake than we knew what to do with. We each got to enjoy our fill of licking, biting, and suckling the chocolate off of each other. My favorite was the nipples. Chocolate covered nipples should be considered a delicacy—one I would happily indulge in any time.

Of course I didn't mind the chocolate infused blow job I received either. Eve licking off the frosting was as enjoyable as I expected, but the way she licked small bites of cake off of me was surprisingly mind blowing. Maybe it was the way her lips raked along the sensitive skin of my cock, or maybe it was the way her tongue swirled the pieces into her mouth, or the combination of both along with the suction of her mouth... it didn't matter. All that mattered was how good it felt, how much fun we both had, and how satisfying our orgasms were.

We could barely stay awake long enough to shower off a second time. I wrapped my arms around her, cradling her against my body as she drifted off to sleep. I'd woken up that morning as a single man and I was falling asleep married. I woke my fiancée up with my face between her thighs and sent her off to sleep three orgasms later.

I hoped our honeymoon was a lot like our wedding day.

Chapter 17
~Eve~

"See that tree over there? The massive one with the little trees all around it? There should be a small offshoot of the falls just on the other side," I called up to Jake who was about ten feet ahead of me with the backpack.

He looked back with a devilish grin on his face and a mischievous twinkle in his eyes. "You sure about this, babe?"

Oh I was sure. My idea to tease Jake had gone better than planned. He'd acted like it wasn't bothering him, but the minute we landed on Guadaloupe the questions started. The man who had just been so calm and cool on the little commuter plane suddenly turned into a talk show host asking question after question.

But I held out. I simply smiled each time he tried to squeeze my ideas out of me. It drove him crazy. Until this morning. He was just starting to stir and the morning light was just starting to stream in through the picture window above our bed when I whispered in his ear.

"Today we're hiking up to the top of the volcano to see the first stage of the waterfalls."

He smiled and stretched with his eyes still closed. "Sounds like fun."

"And you'll fuck me while we're up there."

His eyes shot open and his strong arms tightened around me. "Yes, ma'am!"

Then he was out of bed and digging out his backpack and sneakers before I could even roll over. "We still need to eat breakfast..."

He looked up at me with such serious eyes and pointed at the porch. "Then get eating! I have a challenge to complete!"

I grinned like an idiot all through breakfast.

Every morning a tray of food and coffee was delivered to our porch. It was kind of magical to wake up to fresh fruit and croissants every day. My father's best friend offered up his vacation house on the French-Caribbean island of Guadaloupe for us to escape. It was perfectly located on the rainforest side of the island, which meant we were a five minute car ride from the beach or hiking, depending on which way we turned when we got to the main road.

Jake still hadn't told me what he'd packed in that backpack or how he planned on accomplishing his task, but I didn't care. It was fun to watch Jake. He was like an excited kid and that glint in his eyes every time he looked at me... that was precisely what I was hoping for when I brought the game up in the first place.

"Oh, baby. This is going to be fun..." Jake groaned as he pulled to a stop at a set of small falls that ended in a pool of water, surrounded by forest. We were fairly high up on the dormant volcano and had timed our hike to leave between the scheduled tours, not that many tourists were hiking. Most were more than happy to take the easy walk up to the second stage of the falls and enjoy the view from there. Only a select few chose to make the much harder extra hike the rest of the way up.

It was like we were alone in the world.

The volcano was covered in fairly dense rainforest which made it seem even more intimate. The tree canopy blotted out most of the sunlight and the humidity was incredible. When it rained, it was light, like a mist.

It was so humid my hair had become naturally curly for the first time in my life and I was enjoying the unexpected change, wearing it down in soft waves. At the moment those waves were plastered to the side of my head.

"It looks like we can walk out on those rocks if you want to get closer to the falls," Jake said.

I nodded and waited while Jake took off the backpack and set it against a tree before taking my hand and leading me out onto the wide, flat rocks.

We stopped at the last one I could reach, and Jake wrapped me up in his arms. "It is so beautiful up here."

I nodded as I looked out at the rushing water. "It doesn't look real. The colors are so rich!"

Jake was looking everywhere but at me and that was when I realized he was scouting out a place for us to have fun. I'd been watching for other hikers the whole time, but we never saw anyone. I was really hopeful we'd be alone on our hike for a while longer.

Long enough to have an amazing orgasm under the rainforest canopy.

I'd been on pins and needles all morning. Every sense was tuned to Jake and his body. So when he wrapped his arm around my waist and held me close, it wasn't just his warmth and firm body I felt. I heard every breath and the thud of his heart. I felt the excited energy running under his skin. The anticipation was driving him.

But it was the life in his green eyes that really tugged at my heart. I loved seeing him so happy and light. He grinned and turned me slightly to the right. "There, those bushes next to the pool."

There was a low stand of bushes just in the shade of the trees above. It might work. "We should take a closer look."

Jake threaded his fingers through mine, drawing me along with him as he returned to the shore and retrieved his backpack. This was what I wanted: fun and excitement with Jake. But now that it was here, I was nervous.

Luckily Jake wasn't. He was completely focused on his mission and utterly adorable. It was impossible to not get swept up in his sexy confidence.

The bushes were tall and thick enough that no one would see us unless they came right up on us, which we would ideally hear well in advance. "What do you think Mrs. Spencer?" He was right at my ear and his warm breath danced along my sensitive skin. He tossed the backpack down and wrapped his arm around my waist, pulling my backside flush against his front. "Have I mentioned how much I liked your game idea?"

I laughed as I closed my eyes and leaned into his embrace. Jake's other hand had traveled down between my legs. "I was getting that impression. What's in the bag or is it a secret still?"

He spun me in his arms so that we were face to face. I couldn't help myself; I threw my arms around his neck and kissed him hard. After a long, deep kiss Jake pulled back with an enormous grin on his face. "I'm getting the impression you're enjoying the game, too."

We'd barely started and I was having the time of my life. "A game I can't lose? Oh, I'm having fun."

"You know, I hadn't thought of it that way. It really is a win all around."

I nodded slowly as Jake stepped away to open the mysterious backpack. "Put this around your shoulders, please." He held out an enormous checked blanket. While I wrapped it around my shoulders like a giant, long shawl Jake repositioned me with my back to the water. Then, he kneeled in front of me, kissing my belly and wrapping his large hands around my waist, holding me close.

Standing like that, I imagined I looked like a swimmer drying off. Jake was completely hidden in front of me. He was my secret.

He slid his fingers around the button of my pants, slid the zipper down, and slowly removed my pants. But it was the way he did it—so slowly and lovingly. He studied my skin with his eyes and fingers, moving me where he wanted me with gentle moves. And when he looked up at me from his knees with those soft green eyes I was already so turned on I was finding it hard to stand. My head was spinning.

"Step out," he whispered hoarsely. That was when I realized Jake was panting and a little shaky, too. The moment was affecting both of us.

Underneath my pants and thin white t-shirt I was wearing a bikini. Jake smiled wickedly as he played with the edges of the fabric, but I couldn't keep my eyes on him. The electricity shooting over my skin from his touch was overwhelming. I closed my eyes and ran my hands through his hair as his fingers moved under the fabric.

"My, my, my... so turned on for me, Mrs. Spencer. I like this very much." I peeked down at him hidden in the folds of my blanket. My husband was thoroughly pleased with himself.

"You've got me turned on, now what are you going to do Mr. Spencer?"

He bounced his eyebrows. "Win."

I sucked in an excited breath and tugged on a fistful of hair. Jake laughed deep in his chest as he slid two fingers slowly inside me.

I shuddered and groaned.

"Quiet, please. This is supposed to be a secret..." he chastised me.

I shook my head and smiled with my eyes closed. "Oh shut up and make me come you cocky bastard."

He took my challenge, plunging those long fingers of his deep inside me a split second before he kissed my clit through the fabric. The combination was explosive and revved me up from aroused to verging on climax.

But I wanted more.

I let him work his magic until I was hot and breathless. "I think you should lie down," I whispered.

Jake's green eyes shot up to meet mine, followed by a slow grin.

He eased his fingers out then grabbed a towel from his backpack, wiping his fingers dry before laying it out on the forest floor. "Keep the blanket," he said while bouncing his eyebrows.

Unlike me, Jake had opted for a simple pair of bright green swimming trunks and a t-shirt. He pulled the Velcro apart, allowing his erection to spring free.

It was beautiful and all mine. I straddled him, lowering down to my knees and sinking slowly onto his cock while he held my bikini bottoms to the side and out of the way. He groaned and I placed a finger over his lips, "Now, now. This is a secret, remember?"

But instead of answering me, Jake sank his fingers in to my hips and encouraged me to start moving. "And quick," he reminded me with another quiet moan.

And we were. No one ever came by, it was me and Jake and pure sexual ecstasy. I worshipped him, running my greedy hands over every muscle I could find, enjoying every ridge of his abs and the way our bodies looked coming together. I loved bracing my hands around his flexed biceps as we moved. And I really loved the strain of his neck and shoulders as we came together.

We lay on the ground panting for a few minutes, laughing because well, we'd been successful. Sex— good sex—on a hike in the forest. I was on a high.

"Ready for a swim?" Jake asked, brushing a stray hair from my cheek with his knuckles.

"I'd love one."

The water was actually warm on one end thanks to the volcano and the swim was almost therapeutic. "Is this for real?" I asked as I realized we'd been swimming alone in a hidden paradise for the last hour.

"If it isn't, please don't shatter my dreams."

I smiled and swam into my husband's arms. He pulled me into his lap and nuzzled my ear before kissing me on the cheek. "Happy honeymoon, Jake."

He tensed, tilting my chin up so he could look into my eyes. He had the sweetest smile on his face.

"Happy honeymoon, Eve."

Chapter 18
-Jake-

Eve was making me crazy. Her secret sex list was all I could think about. Every time she came near me I wondered if she was about to whisper something else in my ear. Four days and she'd done it twice—both times were amazing, I might add. Sex in the forest had been nothing short of mind-blowing, but then she went and topped it. We rented a jet ski at the resort on the other side of the island, disappeared into a secluded inlet, and had the best oral sex of my life. The image of Eve sucking me off while I laid back on that jet ski was etched into my brain. I was uncomfortably hard just thinking about it. But then we'd switched. Eve spread on a jet ski was more than I could handle. I was lucky I could still stand and walk. That woman was going to kill me.

So, here we were on a tropical island with no worries and no work, and all I could think about was what else she had on her list.

"Please?" I'd already tried commanding and teasing, now I was on to begging.

"Nope," she replied as she read her book. We were sitting on the porch, enjoying the sounds of the morning and our breakfast.

It really did rain regularly. I knew rainforests got their name for a reason... but I was still surprised by the regular drizzle that fell from the trees above. It made cuddling up with Eve a helluva lot easier. It was a total accident that we picked a place that rained every day to spend our honeymoon together.

It was like fate. Me and Eve and rain...

"How can I properly plan to pleasure you beyond your wildest dreams if you keep them from me?"

She grinned without looking away. "You seem to be doing just fine so far, cowboy."

I puffed up a little at the compliment. "Are there really three challenges on your list, or are you just making them up as you go along." I was teasing her on purpose. I knew Eve well enough to know she had a list. She probably made it out before she even brought the game up in the first place.

Evil. She was just *evil*.

"There are actually five."

I groaned. "You are killing me, woman. Killing me!"

She finally turned toward me. "That's the point. You can't tell me you aren't having fun, Jake. I can see how happy you are."

I was my own worst enemy.

I decided to let it go. Instead, I studied my new wife. She had her nose stuck in a book with a small smile on her lips. I wanted to keep her like that forever. I could already feel this little window of time slipping away from us.

Maybe that's sick of me, but when we got back home there would be work and obligations, illnesses and arguments. I didn't want our lives to ever get so bogged down that we couldn't find our way to a moment like this... where nothing else mattered but the wind and the salt water and being together.

Work, friends, and crazy schedules seemed to be conspiring against us more and more often. The bigger my company got, the more I was lured into projects. I loved my job and being damn good at it was so satisfying, but I wanted more of a hands-off approach. I wanted to oversee and tell other people what to do. I'd quickly slipped down a slope and gone from invisible boss to hands-on employee.

I wasn't so sure I was happy with that change.

On the one hand, I was using my talent and creating a successful business. But on the other hand, my life was getting so busy and complicated, I was frustrated. If I couldn't find a middle ground I was going to go crazy.

"You are lost in thought..." Eve drawled. I was so lost in my head I'd missed her getting up. She slid her hand along my bare abs and chest before sitting sideways in my lap. I could tell by the look in her eyes she was thinking dirty thoughts.

"True enough. I'm sorry." I wrapped my arms

around her and we sat just like that for a while.

"You know the best cure for thinking too much?"

I shook my head knowing exactly where she was going—at least I thought I did.

"Sex."

Yep, exactly what I thought.

"Stop thinking, Jake."

I loved it when Eve was motivated. "Now?"

She nodded slowly with one of those mischievous grins on her face before standing up and grabbing my hand.

I followed Eve as she walked over to the little couch. Her hips swayed as she walked and I zeroed in on the little hint of skin that peeked out the bottom as her shirt as she moved.

God, I loved her ass.

She pushed me down onto the couch, standing over me with her hands on her hips. "What's on your mind?"

I shrugged my shoulders and grinned up at her, "I can't seem to remember at the moment."

She arched her eyebrow and pursed her lips, but didn't smile.

My heart rate skyrocketed.

"Tell me..." she drawled.

I was so turned on I was honestly finding it hard to think of anything but the hint of Eve's nipples under the white t-shirt. "Come here." I wanted to touch her. My brain was going haywire having her so far away.

"Not until you tell me what's got you so upset."

She honestly looked worried and that brought me a little bit of focus. Not much... but a little.

"Something about life and work," I saw Eve's muscles tense at the mention of work so I hurried up my explanation. "You know, philosophizing about the meaning of life."

She relaxed a little, but the focus of her eyes was still intense. She stepped up to me, her knees brushing mine. I was too large for the little couch. My knees were jacked up a good two inches even when I was sitting all the way back in the seat. But Eve trailed a finger down my bare shoulder and over my chest and there was nothing I could do to stop my body from relaxing and leaning back against the cushions no matter how small the seat.

"Think you could get those boxers out of my way?"

I think I broke the land speed record getting that tiny bit of fabric off of my body.

"Excellent," she said with a sexy grin.

I swallowed because I was so damn excited my whole body was vibrating. I loved never knowing what she was going to do next.

Eve kneeled down in front of me, pushing my legs open and licked her lips. Watching her tongue move was almost as good as feeling it on my skin.

Almost.

She leaned in with her hands first and that initial contact of her palms against my cock and naked thigh was enough to shoot me from aroused to fully erect. My blood was pumping so hard I felt lightheaded for a moment.

Then her warm tongue stroked up my length as she wrapped her hand around me and paused, "What else were you thinking about?"

She. Was. Evil.

Eve quite literally had me in the palm of her hand, looking up at me seductively, with that look that said *I will make you come so hard you will forget your own name.* All I had to do was confess—but that was easier said than done.

"I was thinking about how much I resent it when work takes over." I ran my hands through her hair as her eyes softened.

"Keep talking," she whispered and started to move her hands up and down.

I groaned and closed my eyes for a second, enjoying myself and trying my hardest to focus. "You work hard, I work..." my voice fell away as her lips kissed the tip of my cock.

"You work *hard*," she whispered.

Her breath felt so good... "And I'd rather work hard on you," I finished.

She stopped and I felt her grin a split second before she pulled back and said, "Well, you should do that."

I grabbed her and swung her up into my arms. "Let the record show," I said as I stepped back inside, "you asked for it."

Eve was laughing and breathless all the way up until I entered her. All I heard after that was the sound of her calling my name.

It turned out to be a good morning.

Chapter 19
~Eve~

I was so satisfied it was ridiculous. Honeymoons were awesome. It was like a reward for putting up with the complications of a relationship. Rewards were nice.

After all these years I could honestly say I was in love with Jake and we were happy. That was it. No "but" or "except" or "if only..." There were no ex-lovers or business deals. No crappy childhoods or demons to slay. My heart wasn't broken.

Just happy.

I probably would have saved myself some heartache over the years if I'd let myself realize how heartbroken I really was over Jake's disappearance. But instead, I'd buried it down deep and covered it up with a mask of strength. Strength was good, but it didn't fix the broken crack underneath. And because I denied that heartache for so long I let a lot of other things take the brunt of my pain.

It was only now, with my heart so happy, that I realized what Sebastian was telling me that night at the party. He was angry and I was embarrassed so it was hard to hear his words at the time, but I'd had a while to think about it since then. He said there was always a wall I was hiding behind, and he was right. I didn't want to feel my broken heart so I ignored it. I was hiding from my pain and my broken heart, pretending it didn't exist. But pretending doesn't fix things, it only makes them last longer.

I wasted more years than I'd realized in hiding.

It felt good to be free. I hoped I wouldn't make the same mistake twice. I couldn't ever let myself hide again.

"Spill it. What's going on?" Jake asked.

I realized I'd been staring at the wall. "What do you mean?"

Jake glared at me. We were sitting on the porch watching the sun set above the trees. It was beautiful outside and the sunset was casting everything in a pinkish glow. "You've been gone all afternoon—and not in a good way. You look upset."

I took a small sip of the water I was holding and eyed him. He had his determined face on. It was really, *really* unlikely I would convince him to talk about it later. Not that it was going to stop me from trying. I didn't want to talk about heavy stuff when we were having so much fun. "Any chance I could interest you in some sex?"

Jake scoffed, crossed his arms, and propped his

feet up on the little wicker coffee table that matched the chairs and bannister. "You must be deep in that head of yours if you're obviously deflecting with sex."

I stared at him.

He stared at me.

We were in a stare-off and I had a feeling I was going to lose.

"I'm not moving, Eve. I'm not letting anything derail our fun, not even your brain."

I swore under my breath and looked back out at the horizon. Jake was such a pain in the ass sometimes.

"Excuse me?" he asked. "I couldn't hear you over the sarcasm. If you are gonna swear at me, please do it loud enough so I can hear you and properly defend myself."

I glared at him and set my water back down. Loudly. "You are such a cocky bastard sometimes. It pisses me off."

He grinned from ear to ear, his white teeth popped against the tan on his skin and his eyes flashed. "It's not cocky when you're confident, darlin'."

"I think we're talking semantics when it comes to you," I muttered.

"Talk," he said it louder this time. "Or we will have sex."

I perked up at that idea. But then I saw Jake's scowl and realized it wasn't a good thing.

"Oh no, Eve. You won't like this sex. It will be the slow, torturous kind where I try to pull every last detail out of you and won't let you come until I get all the sordid details of what is going on in that head of yours."

Damn it all... he was using my own move against me. Why did I marry such a cocky, demanding, asshole? I was my own worst enemy.

"Please?" he added with a very soft smile that made my heart flutter.

Oh, that's right. Because he was probably the sweetest, most caring bastard I'd ever met. I took a deep breath, closed my eyes, and blurted it out. "I was thinking about my mistakes."

Jake's eyebrows shot up with surprise. "Mistakes?"

I nodded and sighed. We were having this conversation whether I liked it or not. "Don't worry about it. I just got all contemplative. It must be all the relaxing we're doing."

He sat forward. His brows were pulled together with real concern, which only made me love him more. He genuinely cared about me, I'd never doubt that. "Contemplating? What mistakes? Talk to me."

"Seriously, Jake. It's not a big deal! I just..." I sighed, blowing my hair out of my eyes and shaking my head. "I just realized how happy I am right now and how not happy I was for the last ten years because I couldn't admit to myself I was heartbroken."

Jake's face fell. I hated how talking about *me* managed to hurt *him* in the process. It was the last thing I wanted to do, but there was no other way to talk to him. "I'm so sorry, Eve."

"No. This isn't about you or how the last ten years went down. I'm simply evaluating something about myself I want to change in the future. I was an idiot. I refused to deal with my feelings for you and that led me to be less that ridiculously happy. Driven? Yes. Focused and successful? Absolutely. But *happy?* Not completely. Definitely not satisfied."

Jake studied me with those beautiful green eyes of his and I wanted to run my hands along the stubble on his jaw, pull him into my arms, and kiss his lips. But I stayed where I was.

"You weren't happy?"

"I was. I just wasn't as happy as I could have been. I could have been more open and let the past go, but I didn't. I held on to it and used it as an excuse any time I got scared. I don't want to ever do that to myself again. So while we're sitting here relaxing, I took a few minutes to evaluate my life and make some resolutions. Nothing more, nothing less."

The muscle in Jake's jaw flexed a few times as he burned a hole through me with his eyes. "You promise that's all it is?"

I was in his lap in under two seconds, straddling him and wrapping my arms around his neck. "Promise." I kissed him, wrapping my hands around his face and sliding my tongue against his while I squeezed my thighs around his waist. "I'm ready for one of *my* challenges," I breathed between kisses. It turned out Jake's challenges were really rather sweet. He told me honeymoons were for romantic adventures, not hardcore porn. His list was a nonstop roll call of sweet sexual fantasies like making love in a bubble bath and sex under the stars.

Jake grinned up at me, "Which item would you like to check off tonight, Mrs. Spencer? Perhaps sex under the stars?"

I tightened my fingers as he pulled me down against his quickly hardening erection. "Yes, please."

I felt him smile against the skin of my neck, "Your wish is my command."

Chapter 20
-Jake-

Two days later Eve was in the shower and I was back on the porch listening to the rain, thinking about how I'd gotten to where I was right then. I wasn't so sure I'd be sitting on an island in the Caribbean with an amazing, sexy woman who loved me and married me if I hadn't gone through all the shit along the way. I certainly wouldn't appreciate it like I did. I knew that much about myself.

As much as it sucked, I learned something from each and every shitty situation along the way. It either taught me a lesson or gave me a skill. I learned who I was by how I handled those situations. In a lot of ways I felt like I only got to truly see myself for who I was inside when things were at their worst. When the rain was pouring the hardest, the wind was howling, the lightning was everywhere—those were the times when I really knew who I was. It was like the rain storm took everything I thought or believed, washed away the lies and the crap, and showed me what was left—for better or worse.

Some of those times it was nearly impossible to accept what I saw in that reflection. I hated the years when I languished and let life pass me by. I never wanted to be the guy who didn't take his life head-on. But that was exactly who I was back then.

It was only when I had the courage to look at myself that I realized I hated what I saw. I changed it and I liked who I was a helluva lot better now, but it took all of that to get to where I was.

I wondered what role Ashley played in all of that. She probably dragged me down a lot of the time, but I don't know if I would have realized what I wanted without her. She was me in a lot of ways. Broken and clawing to survive, but she was a taker. She liked the pain.

I didn't.

I wanted to leave my past in the past. She made it easy to see what I didn't want.

My mind was buzzing and one of the only ways I knew to calm it down was to write. I'd already grabbed my black journal out of my luggage. It only took a minute before the words started to flow. Sometimes it was hard to get started, but once I did, I couldn't stop. Everything that was so mixed-up in my head would start to unravel, and piece by piece, my mind would clear.

I was so lost in my thoughts I didn't hear the shower stop or Eve come out to stand across from me, so I jumped when she said, "Hey."

"Hey," I said back.

She was studying me very carefully. I could feel the uneasiness in her mood. She moved in front of one of the wicker chairs and carefully sat down. She had a towel in one hand that she was using to dry her hair. "What are you doing?"

She had her eyes fixated on my journal.

"Writing," I said casually.

"Is everything ok?"

I snapped the book shut, set it down on the table, and leaned forward. "Not everything in these journals is bad, Eve. I write to work things out." I moved the journal around unconsciously as I spoke. "It helps me think."

"What are you writing about?" she asked.

I shrugged, hoping it made things seem less intense. Because to me, they felt intense. "Order of events."

Her eyebrows shot up, "What?"

I chuckled and patted the cushion beside me. "Come over here and let me explain."

Eve reluctantly moved across and I turned to the side so she could sit between my legs. I massaged her neck and shoulders while I talked. "You'll hear me out?"

She tensed a little, I massaged harder. "Sure."

I gave her a moment before I dove in. I knew how it was going to sound, but I didn't know how else to phrase things. "I was going over some things and realized I wouldn't be here with you now without the tough times in between." Eve nodded slowly and turned to the side to glance up at me.

I smiled and kept talking. "I know how much you hate Ashley, and I totally get it." I clamped down on her shoulders when she tried get up. "Please, let me explain."

She huffed and stopped fighting me, but crossed her arms over her chest in defiance. "Make it fast."

"I know how much you hate her," I continued. "And as much as I wish I could erase those years that took me away, I don't know how else I'd get to being this man. And like it or not, it took losing control, getting mad, and getting lost, to find my way out. In a weird way, she helped me see who I didn't want to be."

"I really think I need to stomp around or run a mile or something," Eve said through clenched teeth. Every muscle in her body was tensed.

But there was no way I was letting her go. This wasn't something I wanted stewing between us. I wrapped my arm around her chest and leaned down to whisper in her ear. "We have to be able to talk about the past, Eve. Otherwise you are giving it power it doesn't deserve."

She swore under her breath. "Fine."

"All I wanted to do was tell you how much I appreciate the past for bringing me to this moment."

She stewed while I massaged. "I understand what you are saying. I don't like it, but I don't want to argue about it either. I love that we're where we are now, but if that woman is in our lives much longer we're going to have problems."

I couldn't agree more. But as I was sitting there with her, it occurred to me, probably for the first time, everything about Eve that makes me so attracted to her was probably exactly what was going to drive me crazy. I loved that she was smart and successful. It was hot, actually. Eve could take care of herself, so the fact that she wanted me, and let me know all her insecurities, it made that male part of my brain go a little wild. And it made my overprotectiveness kick into overdrive because when Eve *did* need me, it was for a damn good reason. One I'd do anything to fix.

I'd done my time and made my peace with life, but that didn't necessarily mean Eve was in the same place. She was successful, yes, but what if she wanted more? Her career was a huge part of her life, it was very possible she had big plans for what she still wanted to accomplish. I was ready to start winding down, but we could very well be in two totally different places. And that thought sucked.

I was so caught up in the dream of marrying Eve and getting the life I wanted, I didn't really stop and consider what the next ten or twenty years would really look like. I was starting to realize the work wasn't over—it was just beginning.

"Now," I said, pushing aside my weird thoughts. "I really, really want to show you how much I love you. If you're up for it."

Everything about Eve's mood changed in an instant. "Up for what, exactly?"

I had her. "I was thinking about those little words you whispered in my ear this morning."

She gasped and craned her neck to look up at me. "Do you really think you're up for the challenge?"

Chapter 21
~Eve~

There was a sparkle in Jake's eyes. It could only mean one thing: trouble.

"Two minutes, Eve. I *know* I can get you off in less than two minutes."

I arched a very skeptical eyebrow. "No you can't."

His answering grin was enormous. "Oh, yes I can." He moved closer and leaned down so that our noses were touching. "And I'm gonna prove it..."

Then he ran the back of his knuckles along my cheek at the same time he lowered his eyes and kissed me. My whole body groaned for more of whatever the hell it was Jake had just done to me. Knuckles and lips... in just the right way, and just the right time, were apparently magic.

He smiled at me lazily and cocked his head so he could whisper in my ear. "Please. I want to do dirty, dirty things to you Mrs. Spencer." He kissed the spot behind my ear and I sighed. "I want to bury my fingers inside you while you look out at the forest and moan so loudly every other person here on vacation wishes they were you."

I was so wet it was ridiculous. Just words... they were just words... my body wanted all those words.

Damn body.

Jake trailed his fingers over my chest and stomach, stopping short of my bikini bottoms. "Please? Let me?"

I'm pretty sure my legs fell open. I was a puppet and he was the master. He said a few magical words and my legs did as he wished. It didn't matter that I hadn't thought about sex since I whispered in his ear that morning. It didn't matter that two minutes ago I was as far from turned on as a person could get. Jake had worked me over and I wanted what he was offering.

He grinned and his green eyes flashed. I couldn't help myself, I reached out and ran my fingertip through the dip of his dimple and kissed it a split second before his fingers pressed against my sex. "Two minutes, starting now." He was holding up his wrist so I could look at his watch, not that I was really paying much attention to the hands on the watch. My mind was pretty fixated on the hands touching my body.

His fingers slid inside me without any effort at all. I was that wet. He groaned, "Oh, I'm gonna need to taste that..." He slid his long fingers in and out several times before pulling away and licking them clean. I could really care less how much he did or didn't like the way I tasted, all I could think about was how empty I felt without him inside me. I was throbbing. I think that was exactly what the cocky bastard wanted too, because he waited for me to look at him before he pulled his fingers out of his mouth and thrust them back inside me with a wicked grin.

I gasped and threw back my head. He could do whatever the hell he wanted to me. And he could take as long as he wanted to—I wouldn't give him any grief for going over his two minutes.

While Jake did magical things inside my body he ran his other thumb over the exposed parts of my breast, inching closer to my covered nipples, but not going near them. He was teasing me.

"Do you know what it does to me to feel how wet you are for me? Do you have any idea how much control you have over me, Eve?" I forced my eyes open because I knew he wanted me to look at him when he poured his soul out to me. His eyes locked onto mine. "I live for these moments. I will do anything you want. Ask me for anything, and I will give it you."

He thrust deeper inside me at the same time his thumb ran over my nipple beneath my swimsuit. I couldn't catch my breath. It was gone and my body was wound up, every muscle tensed, as I gasped for air. "You are so fucking beautiful when you let me have you."

I shuddered as his breath danced along my neck and I came completely undone, coming around his fingers as he pressed into me. He kissed my neck up and down as I cried out his name, my toes curling and hips tilting into his fingers. "So beautiful," he whispered, which only intensified the end of my orgasm. Knowing how Jake felt about me was always a huge turn on.

When I finally relaxed, he pulled his fingers away, licking and glancing down at his watch. "Two minutes on the nose."

I sat up and grabbed his wrist, twisting his watch so I could see it better. "No..."

"Yes..." he chuckled.

Sure enough, as best I could remember, it had been exactly two minutes since he showed me the time. "That is some raw talent, Jake. I wish we could harness it for something useful."

He used a towel to finish wiping his hand clean and leaned over my body, "I can't think of anything more useful than giving you pleasure at any time and place."

I think I may have blushed under his intense stare. It was probably the hottest look I had ever seen. Ever. "Well, then. When you put it like that..."

He nodded and kissed me. "Excellent. Now, your turn."

My turn? What the hell did that mean? I hadn't agreed to anything other than the two-minute challenge.

Jake laughed and shook his head. "Oh no. It's not what you're thinking." He stood up and pulled the other chair over, positioning it so he was facing me when he sat back down. "Same deal. Can you get *yourself* off in two minutes?"

Me? "I just got off. That's not fair."

He crossed his arms and looked at me pointedly. "Don't think you can do it, huh?"

Ass. "I'm just saying it isn't fair. Round two can take time..."

"Or it can happen twice as fast since you're already hot and bothered."

"Therefore, it is an unfair test."

He shrugged his shoulders and looked away. "I guess I know your body better than you do."

He did *not* just say that out loud. "Excuse me?"

"You heard me," he laughed. "I am saying I think I know your body better than you do. I want you to prove me wrong."

I stared at him for a full minute before I decided there wasn't really anything to lose by proving him right. He knew my body better than I did and we both knew it but, in the meantime, I'd get another orgasm while I drove my new husband absolutely wild. I slid my bikini tops to the side, exposing my breasts as I spread my legs back open. "Start the clock."

Jake swallowed hard as he barely glanced at his watch, "Go."

By the time I was done moaning it had been three minutes. I wasn't sad to lose that bet because in those three minutes I got to watch Jake lose his mind. He begged and pleaded and practically ripped the arms off the chair. He was torturing himself but, he'd asked me to do it.

Three minutes of exquisite torture later, I had two orgasms and he had none. But because I was feeling like having more fun, I stood up and stripped off my bikini before beckoning him inside to the bedroom where I let him have me hard against the bed.

***

I was a tangled mess in the white sheets and Jake was lying on his back beside me as the morning light filtered in through the open windows. By the rhythm of his breathing and the way he had his arms propped up behind his head, I knew he was awake. It had become a new favorite sleeping position for us—my back pressed to his side. Sometimes he turned and spooned me, but for the most part, Jake had been sleeping on his back.

I shifted and stretched, loving the feel of the strange sheets as they moved over my naked skin.

"Mornin' darlin'," Jake drawled sleepily. "Did you sleep well?"

"Mmmm," I replied. My eyes were still closed and I wasn't quite ready to form words.

He chuckled. His voice was deep and rough from sleep. "I think breakfast is waiting for us. Do you want it in bed today?"

I shook my head and stretched again before rolling over to lie on his broad chest. "No, just give me a minute. I like eating on the porch."

Jake stroked his fingers up and down my back

while I woke up. He was so quiet I had to wonder how long he'd been awake.

"How about you?" My voice was muffled against his chest.

"I slept great, actually. I think I've slept better here than anywhere I've ever slept." He ran his fingers through my hair. "The longer we're away from home, the more it feels like a different life. You've changed too, you know."

"True," I was calmer than ever. "How long have you been awake?"

Jake shrugged, "A while."

"And what have you been doing?" I looked up at him with one eye open. He was damn sexy in the morning with stubble on his chin and messy hair.

"Listening to you breathe, and of course all your secrets. You really shouldn't talk so much in your sleep."

"I don't talk in my sleep," I scoffed. "I should know, I lived with the nosiest sister on the planet. She'd have told me if I unwittingly divulged secrets in my sleep."

"Well, it's that... or she just kept her best source of information a secret."

I punched him lightly in the side and pushed up onto my elbow. "What have you really been doing?"

Jake ran his thumb along my cheek and brushed my hair over my shoulder all while studying me with the softest look on his face. "Honestly, nothing. I've just been enjoying *this*."

I could see the lie in his eyes, but I let it go.

Whatever was on Jake's mind, it wasn't worth pushing my new husband on our vacation. "Coffee?"

Jake grinned. "After you."

I pulled the spare sheet off the chair where I'd been storing it each night, and wrapped it around my body. My hair was everywhere and I didn't even bother to tame it before I followed Jake out onto the porch. Two trays filled with coffee, juice, croissants, and fruit were waiting for us, as usual.

I arranged myself on the chairs with my feet propped up while Jake served the coffee. It was the quietest breakfast and I think we were both dreading the next stage of our lives: going back to reality. Neither one of us wanted to talk about it, but we couldn't stop thinking about it.

Everything up until that point had been easy, reactionary. Falling back in love was intense and left little time for worrying about anything else. We were going to have to think and plan, agree and compromise. What we were heading home to was a complete unknown.

Especially when I added *her* into the equation. Jake was true to his word. He hadn't pulled his phone out once and Greg hadn't called the house, so what was happening while we were away was a complete mystery. I was happy about that until I realized we were going home blind. Anything could be waiting for us. I hated surprises.

Jake was staring off into the bushes surrounding the porch, absent-mindedly pulling off strips of croissant and popping them in his mouth.

Where would we be in five years? Would he still be as handsome? Would he still love me or would I drive him crazy? Would one of us become so engrossed in work that we forgot how to have fun?

"Promise me," I whispered.

Jake snapped his head around to look me in the eye. "Promise you what?" Then he reached out and slid his long fingers around my hand.

"Promise me you won't let me forget how it feels right now. Don't let me forget." I knew myself well enough to know that once we got back to our lives I would let things like work and worrying about the future cloud my ability to simply live in the moment. I would get swept away.

He studied me intently for a minute. His muscles were rigid and his jaw was clenched. Jake's instinct would be to do something tangible, to take immediate action to solve the problem. Except there was nothing to do. This was exactly why I usually avoided saying things like this, I didn't want to ask him for something that would only frustrate him, but I was desperate. I needed him to understand how frantic and helpless I was feeling in that moment.

"Ok," he said simply and squeezed my hand, but it was the conviction in his eyes that told me how seriously he took my request. "I'm putting it on my list of husbandly responsibilities," he winked and grinned his cocky half-smile.

"My god, Jake Spencer. You may be the hottest husband on the planet," I breathed.

He leaned in, pulling my hand so that I was forced

to turn into him, and kissed me lightly on the lips. "I don't even register on the same scale with you." Then he slid his hands up my arms and grabbed my face, kissing me very, very intently.

I wanted to get lost in that kiss with Jake, but my mind was already betraying me. It was already back home, strategizing and worrying about the potential threats to my marriage, not the least of which was a redhead I needed placed on the first plane out of town.

Chapter 22
-Jake-

"Movie's ready!" Eve called from the living room.

We were having a romantic night in and I was cooking. "Be there in two minutes!" I called back.

The spaghetti was done—I just had to serve everything up. It was hard to believe it was almost over. One more day... and then back to reality. I was dreading it. The last two weeks had been amazing. Nothing in our real lives would ever be as relaxing or fun. It just wouldn't.

I dumped the sauce on top of the noodles, popped in some silverware, and joined Eve on the couch in front of the television.

"Thanks, babe." The lights were off so we were eating by the glow of the movie and the couple dozen candles Eve had placed around the little house. Eve was wearing a t-shirt and not much else. Her hair was pulled into a ponytail over one shoulder and I was kind of hoping the movie sucked so I could strip her naked and make out with her on the couch instead.

"What's it about?"

She grinned, "Explosions and sex. I basically picked something where the words wouldn't matter."

The only movie choices were in French, and since I didn't speak the language, Eve was trying to be helpful. Of course, there was the fact that Eve actually liked movies full of explosions and sex, but that was just nitpicking.

Unfortunately for me, the movie was actually pretty good. I was awake until the very end, while Eve was asleep in my lap. "Movie's over, darlin'," I whispered while I rubbed her back.

"Leave me on the couch, I'm comfy," she groaned and burrowed deeper into my lap.

I sighed because, of course, that oddly felt nice. "I'm not leaving you on the couch."

"You are such a pessimist."

"How am I a pessimist because I don't want to sleep without you?" Eve always came up with the funniest stuff when she was half asleep.

She sat up and looked at me with one eye open. "I don't know. Maybe it makes you an optimist, then?"

I just shook my head and hopped to my feet. Eve took my hand and let me guide her toward the bedroom, which was pretty hard because she wasn't looking where she was going.

"Ow." She walked right into the wall leading to the kitchen.

"It would probably help if you opened your eyes..."

"You are so bossy."

I just shook my head and scooped her up. "I think it's best if I take it from here. You're like a drunk driver, Eve."

"Whatever," she murmured and wrapped her arms around my neck.

She was asleep as soon as I laid her down, but I was wide awake with nothing to do. It was a dangerous combination and, for the first time since our wedding day, I thought about my conversation with my uncle. I'd successfully and very skillfully avoided it every other day. But it was always there in the back of my mind, haunting me.

Tom said a few things that I couldn't get out of my head, the most important being I shouldn't even bother with Ashley. I wanted to chalk up my desire to hear Ashley out to my manners, but I knew it was more than that. I felt an obligation to her, not because of our past, but because I knew what it was like to be haunted.

It was stupid, I knew it was stupid. But I couldn't bring myself to ignore her.

We both had insanely abusive fathers, but mine usually kept his focus on me. Ashley's didn't, and that small difference had led to a chain of events that changed her life forever. Tom was right when he said she was far more damaged than me, but he was wrong about one thing. I was fairly sure if I had killed my father I wouldn't have gotten back up again. He and Eve both seemed to think I had an unwavering ability to pick myself back up after being handed piles of shit.

I thought they were wrong.

Ashley was stronger than me. She was still up and walking around. She was still fighting, even if it didn't seem healthy to everyone else. I was one of only a handful of people who knew Ashley's full story, not even Tom and Greg knew all the details. As far as they were concerned she was like me, shitty childhood, shitty parents.

I hadn't even told Eve. And I wasn't going to. There was the simple fact that she didn't need to know, but there was also a code I didn't want to break. Ashley had allowed me to know all the details and I didn't want to betray that confidence. People like us didn't trust many people with details like that.

You can't unsee those images, even when it is just your imagination putting the details together. And I didn't want to put Eve through that.

Besides, Ashley wasn't going to be around long enough for any of it to matter.

I didn't want to disturb Eve, so I slipped out of bed for some water and to blow out the candles we'd left burning. When I came back I stopped in the doorway and stared at my wife.

Moonlight and candlelight were the only things lighting Eve's soft skin. She was perfection. She was art.

The room was cast in a blue glow, but Eve's skin looked more like the glow of the candles, soft and incandescent. The shadows weren't pure black.

Instead they were shades of grey that gradually morphed into something a shade lighter than black.

I wanted to touch her and see for myself if she was as soft and warm as she appeared, but I didn't want to waste the opportunity in front of me—the chance to see a rare piece of art with my own eyes.

It was like Eve could sense I was restless. She rolled over and looked right at me. "Why are you awake?"

"Thinking."

"What are you thinking?" she asked. Her dark hair was down, delicately resting against that skin I couldn't stop staring at. Her eyes and her smile were soft flashes in the shadows. Every feeling and emotion tied to desire and need inside me was on fire.

"That you are the most beautiful thing I've ever seen."

That's when I heard it. That hitch in her breathing. She only made it when I caught her off-guard. Right at that moment I was so grateful for the silence. No music or rain or anything. Just Eve and me. So I heard it when she sucked it that excited little breath of air and held it.

She swallowed. "I'm looking at something amazing, too."

By reflex I looked down at myself. I was naked except for a pair of boxers that were doing a terrible job of hiding the way I felt about Eve.

The only sound in the room was the softness of her breathing, which drew my eyes to her chest. Her naked breasts were slowly rising and falling with each excited breath. The shadows moved up and down, making her skin look so very soft...

She shook her head while she looked into my eyes. I swear she was reading my mind and finding out all my secrets because a moment later she sighed. "C'mon Romeo. We didn't get movie sex, so we better fool around now and get your mind off your troubles."

"Oh yeah?" I asked.

"Yep. After a good orgasm you should sleep."

"Well, if it is what the doctor orders..." Eve was absolutely my doctor—I swear she even understood the stuff I kept from her. She had some sort of super-empathy that let her understand things she couldn't possibly have any concept of—at least when it came to me.

"I do. I prescribe one orgasm and a good night of sleep. Now be a good patient and fuck me."

"Yes, doctor." I smiled but I didn't move. I couldn't. I needed this memory. Wasting something this perfect would be sacrilege. Besides, I'd learned a little patience went a long way.

"Don't make me wait," she pleaded.

"I'm not making you wait, darlin'. I'm making this count."

She sucked in another soft breath which made every inch of my skin tingle. She closed her eyes and slowly leaned her head back. That was when I saw the slight tremble of her arms and I couldn't resist her for another moment.

I hooked my thumbs inside the waistband of my boxers and pushed them to the floor before climbing onto the bed and moving toward Eve. "Finally," she sighed.

"No," I replied. "Just right."

She shook her head and smiled slowly as she looked up into my eyes. "You are such a tease, Jake Spencer."

"And you, Eve Spencer, are my muse."

It was my turn to suck in a breath. I was completely overwhelmed the moment my skin made contact with hers. Soft. So much softer than I'd hoped. It didn't matter how many times I'd touched Eve's skin, each experience was new and unexpected.

I wanted to be close to her. I wanted her in my arms where I could hold her against me, but I didn't want to take my eyes off of her either. "Turn over for me?"

She grinned and bit the corner of her lip. "I like what you're thinking..."

On her knees, I pulled her body against mine, her back to my front, and eased down until she was sitting in my lap. We were completely connected from head to toe. My erection was sitting against her warm skin, throbbing and begging to be inside her, but I wasn't ready. I was so turned on I wouldn't last long. Besides, it gave me more time to enjoy touching her.

Above our bed was a large picture window and with the candlelight there was just enough reflection to see all the lines and curves of her body. Her belly was soft as I ran my hands across it and up to caress the outsides of her breasts. The sensation was almost too much to handle and I let out an unplanned groan.

"Like what you feel?" she murmured and gasped as my fingers closed around her nipples.

"I want more."

She arched and laid her head back on my shoulder, giving me complete access to her body. I continued to tease her nipples, rolling and pulling as she moaned and writhed. "Bend over," I whispered in her ear when I couldn't take it anymore. I needed to be inside her.

She moved forward onto her hands and knees. Her back was arched so that the shadows stretched across her skin, calling for me to touch her again. I ran my hands up and down her spine before wrapping them around her hips and slowly pushing my way inside her hot, slick sex.

Eve was panting and moaning my name by the time I completely buried myself inside her. The muscles of her core spasming and contracting around my hard cock and sending wave after wave of overwhelming pleasure through my body.

I buried myself inside her and pulled her ass hard against me as I sank down to my feet and stretched myself out across her back. Eve sighed with satisfaction and rested on her elbows. "I love this position. So close..."

Very close. She was in my arms, pressed completely against me with my cock inside her. It was incredibly intimate.

With one hand wrapped around her waist to hold her as close to me as possible, I slid the other under her breast and began to work it once again. Eve sucked in another excited breath before moaning loudly and shuddering. "More. I want more, Jake."

When she begged like that, all my thoughts and plans went out the window. I followed her commands like a desperate soldier. What she asked for, I gave. If she wanted more, I would give it to her, even if took every ounce of strength inside me. I pumped into her harder and kissed her back, buried my nose in her hair, and ran my teeth along her skin. She cried out, I gave her more, until her hands clenched the sheets in fists, her muscles went rigid, and she yelled out as a powerful orgasm tore through her.

I managed to hold out for a few seconds before it was all too much for me. Her voice, the heat of her skin, and the wetness of being inside her satisfied body were more than I could handle at that angle.

When we were both relaxed and satisfied I still couldn't let her go. I didn't want to move ever again. The night, the glow, and the woman in my arms... it would never get any better than this.

Chapter 23
~Eve~

"Move!" Jake pleaded.

"No." I was not moving. I could starve to death right where I was and die a happy death. No one would blame me. I married the perfect guy, went on a dream honeymoon, and found the absolute most perfect spot on the beach. What else was there?

"Don't make me come after you."

"You wouldn't dare..." I lowered my sunglasses and gave him my most deadly look. But Jake just shook his head at me.

"I've been more than kind to you on this trip, darlin'. Too kind."

"Why can't I skip lunch? We'll eat an early dinner."

"You think I'm going to fall for that? You'll be passed out before two and I'll have to carry you back. It isn't exactly the kind of story I want to tell years from now—the day Eve nearly died from starvation because she was too comfortable to move."

I stuck my tongue out at him and that was the end of things. He dove for me, scooping me up in his arms, walking straight into the chilly ocean.

"You are insane!" I yelled as I lost my breath. The water wasn't chilly—it was fucking cold.

He kissed my cheek, "Maybe, but you are up and out of your chair. A guy's gotta do what a guy's gotta do."

My skin was already going numb. "Can we dry off and go get lunch, then?"

He smiled, his eyebrows bouncing and his dimple showing. "Absolutely. I'm starving."

Jake had fallen in love with this little dive restaurant in a shack (if you could even call it that) on the beach. It served his favorite whiskey and had every kind of seafood imaginable. I was happy because it had food and a view of the beach.

We settled in at the bar, Jake in his trunks and a t-shirt, me with a skimpy sundress over my bikini, and both of us with flip-flops dangling from our toes as we rested our feet against the footrest on the bar.

"Whiskey?" the bartender asked in his thick French accent.

Jake smiled and nodded, he was damn sexy when he smiled with that dimple. I held up two fingers and murmured, "*Deux, sil vous plait.*"

The man chuckled and grabbed the rectangular bottle of Johnny Walker, pouring the strong amber liquid over ice cubes and squeezing a wedge of lime into mine before sliding the glasses toward each of us. "Enjoy." It sounded like two words the way he said it.

The whiskey burned my nostrils as I took a very small sip. Drinking it straight like that was like drinking fire, but it also went straight to my head without a sickeningly sweet aftertaste. I shuddered as I set the glass down. "Damn that's strong…"

"Yep," Jake agreed and ran his hand up my thigh. "I've loved being able to relax and do whatever the hell we feel like, whenever the hell we feel like it."

I had to agree that vacation looked good on Jake. He was like a different person. He never stopped smiling and his eyes… oh god, they were pure sex. When he looked at me with those mischievous green things I was done for, *every single time.* They were hypnotizing and hot, but I had a feeling it also had something to do with the fact he was looking at me like he wanted to do dark, dirty things with every inch of me. It took my breath away every time and I went weak in the knees. Not to mention the deep throbbing between my legs that made me feel like I was about to pass out.

It was our last day and we'd vowed to spend every minute of it on the beach, so after I put food into my body we made our way back to our spot.

The sand was so different from anything I'd ever seen before. It was soft and full of colors from the island's volcano. It made the beach look like it was a deep shade of rich brown, but when I looked closer I realized it was a mix of white, red, black, brown, grey, and probably more. It was beautiful. The beach sloped sharply down to the water, so Jake scooped out makeshift chairs that we laid our towels over.

"Grapes?" Jake asked, holding out the bag.

"I feel like that is starting to become a loaded question around you. Are you going to steal them away and make me kiss you?"

He grinned. "I like to keep things mysterious."

"Hmmm...." I acted like I was seriously thinking while I popped a couple of grapes in my mouth and chewed. "Mysterious, like how and when you plan on accomplishing your final challenge?"

His grin widened. "Oh, I have that all planned out. And it *will* remain a mystery until then."

Three hours later, Jake hit me with a mud ball.

It oozed down my back and plopped onto the sand. "You did *not* just hit me. Did you?"

When I turned around, Jake was grinning. He had a fistful of mud in one hand and the other held out as a shield. The beach was so sloped his left knee was bent while his right was standing straight. "I sure did."

I shook my head, partially because I was shocked, and partially because I wanted desperately to peg him back, but I knew if I didn't plan it right he'd dodge out of the way before I could hit him.

My feet were firmly planted in the wet sand, so I slowly bent down (never taking my eyes off him, the sneaky bastard) and grabbed two fistfuls of mud. I could either fling them at him right away and hope I was faster than him, or I could take the slow approach—confuse him and keep him guessing.

I went with the slow approach, slowly sauntering over until I was looking up at him. "What happened to romance and sex on the beach?"

He was breathing hard as he looked down at me, probably because I'd said "sex" at the same time I'd pushed my breasts up toward his face. "Romance can be fun, too, can't it?"

I nodded slowly, "I suppose. Is a mud fight, *fun*?"

His lips twitched at the corners. "It can be."

I took both handfuls of mud and slapped them against his chest, smearing the wet brown sand over his skin. "You're right, this *is* fun."

He shook his head and dropped his handfuls of mud on the ground, grabbed my face with his filthy hands, and kissed me hard. "You better run, Eve. I'm coming for you!"

I squealed and took off down the beach. Jake was right behind me, I could hear the pounding of his feet on the hard sand. Mud flew by my head as he unloaded, but it all missed me. I was out of breath and laughing so hard I was seeing stars when he caught me, picked me up by circling his arms around my waist from behind, and carried me into the trees.

"What are you doing?" I yelled between gasps.

"Fulfilling my list!" he huffed back, dropping me on the ground beside a blanket and towels.

"What is this?"

His lips were at my ear as he pressed his hips into my backside. "You said you didn't want any sand in unwanted places." That morning I'd woken him up by whispering a final challenge in his ear: sex on the beach that wasn't awkward and didn't hurt. I thought it was impossible but...

I shivered as his breath danced across my skin and I realized exactly what we were about to do. "The real world is seriously going to suck after this," I sighed.

I felt his erection dig into my backside as he groaned, "Did you have to remind me?"

I spun in his arms, throwing my hands around his neck. "Let's have one last crazy adventure, Jake. We'll worry about the future when we get there."

Jake grinned and kissed me. "Just how crazy are we talking?"

I rolled my eyes and pulled him down toward the blanket. "You are insatiable, Jake Spencer."

He rolled on top of me and looked right into my eyes. "You know you love it."

I did. I loved knowing Jake always wanted more. I just needed to keep up with him.

Chapter 24
-Jake-

"Welcome home Mrs. Spencer. You ready for this?"

She smirked at me, "You like asking me that question."

I shrugged, "I like knowing we're both ready to jump. I'd hate to drag you into something you weren't ready for. You and me together, remember?"

"Yep, let's do this cowboy. Back to reality." She was staring at me with the oddest look in her eyes.

"What?"

She shook her head slowly and shrugged her shoulders. "Nothing. We should go inside."

I didn't try to figure out what the hell she was hinting at, I just scooped her up in my arms and opened the front door.

"I don't think it ever gets old," she laughed, running her hands through my hair.

"Walking through doorways?"

"No," she replied. "Getting tossed around by you. How strong are you, exactly?"

I laughed, but every time she said something like that I got all excited. "I can't help that you are so much smaller than me..." whatever else I was about to say died in my mouth because everything inside the house was different.

Were we in the right house?

"Surprise!" Eve shrugged, looking up at me sheepishly.

I set her down before I dropped her. "What is all this?" Boxes were neatly lined up in the living room, the furniture was gone, and the walls had a fresh coat of paint on them.

"It's my other wedding present to you. I thought our new life should start with a home that was both of us."

I felt a little stupid. I knew Eve was talking, but somehow the words weren't quite making sense to me. I walked further into the room so I could see all of it. The cream walls were now a rich shade of gray and the dining room was deep blue.

"I just had them paint these two rooms for now. I noticed your old apartment and your office were both gray and blue... I thought you might like it at home, too."

"Thank you." Those were the only two words I could come up with. I was honestly, truly, dumbfounded.

Had I been more obvious about my feelings

toward the house than I realized? Or did Eve just know me that well? Did it matter? "This means a lot to me..." I finally said, staring at the blank walls.

"You like it? It wasn't silly?"

"God, no. This is..." the words disappeared. I didn't know how to say thank you for making our home more than it already was. "I didn't expect this."

"I know. That's what made it even more fun. You don't ask for anything, Jake. Ever."

I knew she was trying to make a point, but I didn't care. We could talk about it later. All I cared about were the two rooms I was looking at. "Do *you* like blue and gray?"

She laughed and slid her hands around my waist, tilting her head up to look at me. "Of course. I wouldn't have picked colors I hated. I love you, but I *do* have to live here."

I nodded and started picturing where I could put a couple of my things. "Then yes, blue and gray are perfect. Do we have surprise furniture arriving soon?"

She slid her phone out and pulled up her photo album. "Tell me whether you like option A, B, or C. I'm particularly in love with option B."

There were pictures of her and Jennie in a furniture store, lying on couches. Option A was a tan microfiber couch and matching chairs. Option B was a rich brown leather couch with brass grommets. And Option C was an elegant white couch.

"I'm in love with option B, too."

She smiled and took back her phone, bringing up a

contact and hitting "send". "Good," she said smiling up at me. "I was hoping to make the room a little old school and sports themed."

"What about the dining room?" I asked, wondering if I was getting a vote on that as well.

"That is picked by default. I had two options ready depending on which living room option you chose." She held up her hand. "Hey Rick! Thanks.... Yes we're home. He picked option B." There was a pause while she listened to Rick. "Perfect. Yes, everything sounds perfect. Thank you."

She ended the call and slid the phone back into her jeans pocket. "It will be here tomorrow afternoon. Now, before I go crazy and decorate you right out of the house again, pick out anything you want in here. Do whatever you want, change whatever you want to change, I'll come in and finish it up when you're done."

"Can't we do this together? Or is this woman's work and I'm not allowed to really help out?"

She smiled and bounced her eyebrows. "Oh no, we can totally do this together. I just wanted to make sure you had all your options available to you. You know, since you never ask for anything."

There it was again. I ignored her comment. I wasn't letting her bait me into a conversation like that in our first thirty minutes at home. "Let's order pizza and redo our house."

A small look of disappoint flashed in her eyes, but she quickly hid it. "Pepperoni or supreme?"

***

The last thing I wanted to do was turn my phone back on. The second to last thing I wanted to do was get dressed for work. I hadn't been shy at all about my feelings. In fact, I'd been so damn vocal about my disinterest in returning to our old lives I was afraid Eve was going to divorce me.

But ten minutes before my alarm should have gone off, I felt her curling around me, her leg wrapping around mine, and her hands gliding across my bare chest. I brushed back her hair, "You awake?"

She shook her head.

I laughed a little and kept running my fingers through her hair. Once I was awake I couldn't go back to sleep, so instead, I debated getting up and facing the day head-on. But the minute I tried to move, Eve wrapped herself tighter around me like she didn't want me to move. "I'm not going anywhere."

She sighed and burrowed in closer.

Eve didn't want to go back to work any more than I did, she was just going about it differently. I wanted to make new plans and refocus our goals. Eve wanted to debate and think while facing her life. I was an idiot for not realizing how different we were and assuming she wanted to jump back into the heart of her most stressful month at work.

So I decided to stop being the giant man-baby I was being, and make it easier on both of us. I held her close and brushed her hair while I ran my hand up and down her arm and told her a story. "I remember one morning, waking up early just like this. I was dreading the whole day. I didn't want to go to school. I didn't want to think or eat or study. All I wanted to do was get to the end. So, I laid in bed, mad that I couldn't fast-forward time and get to seven o'clock any faster."

"What was going to happen at seven?" she asked sleepily.

I smiled since she couldn't see me. "You'll just have to wait and find out."

I felt her smile against my chest.

I continued, "The whole day was shit. I don't think I heard a single thing my teachers said," I was purposefully using generic words like "teachers" so I could drag out the suspense. "I skipped lunch and moped around... I was useless, but at least I was something to keep me going. I got home and had nothing to do except get worked up. I changed my clothes three times."

"Girl."

"Do you want to hear this story?" I joked back. I waited for her nod. "After I changed for the third time—*like a girl*—I tried on all my hats. Then I practiced what I was going to say in the mirror. I smiled and tested all my looks out until I had it just right. And I still had an hour to kill... so I went out to the field early to practice. Normally I was a show-off, but that night I wanted to be extra awesome."

I think Eve was holding her breath, I didn't really feel her breathing. She had an idea of where this story was going. "Everyone started showing up and I couldn't stop looking around. I mean, this was it. I'd waited all day long for *this*. And then there she was, and all that waiting didn't matter anymore. She brought a friend—which sucked—but she was laughing and smiling, and looked just about as nervous and excited as I was, thank god. I jogged right over to her and kissed her on the cheek. I wanted to kiss her on the fucking mouth, but I didn't want to scare her."

Eve shook her head, "You should have kissed her, I bet she would have kissed you back."

I sucked in a breath. "Seriously? You would have kissed me back? After one date?"

She ran her fingers up my chest and cupped my face. "We kissed twice the night before... why not?"

"We kissed more than twice."

She propped herself up on her elbow, I could just barely make out her outline in the dark. The sun wasn't even close to coming up yet. "No, we kissed twice. Once in the movie theater, and once at my door."

"I kissed you a helluva lot more than once at the door." At least it seemed like it to me.

She shook her head, her hair tickling the skin of my arm. "Nope. It was one fantastic, long, amazing, knock-my-socks-off kiss. And if you had kissed me on the lips the next night at the field, even in front of Jennie, I would have kissed you back. You weren't the only one waiting all day..." she leaned in and kissed me tenderly on the lips. It took my breath away. "But to be perfectly honest, the kiss on the cheek was a brilliant move."

"Brilliant, eh?" I liked the way that sounded. I was pretty bummed, even fourteen years later, to learn I could have just kissed the hell out of her— missed opportunities to have my lips on hers always hurt.

"Mmmm... Jennie thought you were so damn sweet she couldn't stand it. And for that matter, neither could I. Do you know how happy you looked to see me?"

I ran my hand down her arm and around her hip. "I think I have an idea. It was probably pretty close to how ridiculously happy you looked to see me. You were vibrating and your smile was so big... there was no mistaking how you felt. Stephen even joked I was getting lucky that night."

She kissed me again. "You didn't get lucky, but it was a pretty special night."

I sighed and pulled her lips against mine again. They were simple morning kisses, but they were still sexy. I turned her head to the side and kissed her ear, "A very special night."

"You remember?" I couldn't believe she actually sounded surprised.

I rolled her underneath of me, she opened her legs so I could settle between them and kissed up her neck, "Darlin', a man doesn't forget the night he stakes his claim on the woman he wants. That was the night you said you'd be mine and I knew I had to go after you with everything I had."

Her nails lightly scored my skin as she ran them up my arms and across my shoulders, tilting her hips up to grind against mine. "No regrets about that decision?" she was joking and begging me to show her exactly how happy I was to be her husband.

"The only thing I regret about that night, is not kissing you on the lips."

She gasped as I wrapped my arm around her waist and began nudging my cock against her sex. She arched her back to accommodate me and wrapped her arms around my shoulders for leverage. Her skin against mine felt amazing, but my cock pressing into her warm and clearly aroused body was mind numbing. "You can make it up to me by giving me an orgasm before heading back to reality."

I gave her a fucking mind-blowing orgasm, one that had her smiling all the way out the front door with her coffee in one hand and her work bag in the other. I followed her out the door and to the interstate where we went our separate ways. Every second I drove, I could physically feel the distance between us growing. I tried to comfort myself with the fact that I could still drop in and surprise her any time. We could still meet for lunch and she could still come surprise me at work. We had a good life here. We both had good jobs with enough seniority we could make our schedules fairly flexible.

But it wasn't enough. Not for me.

Fuck, it wasn't even close to enough.

I was so far up inside my head when I walked into work I almost skipped saying hello to Lisa and the rest of the staff, all of whom were waiting for me with ridiculous grins and lots of congratulations. "That was the most romantic wedding I have *ever* been to!" Lisa gushed.

"Thank you," I replied. I really didn't know what else to say to that. It wasn't like I was going to talk about the lighting and flower arrangements.

"I've never seen two people so in love. You two are just perfect," she said and grabbed a tissue. "I'm so happy for you, boss."

I rolled my eyes and hugged her. "I really appreciate that." Which I did. I wasn't good at accepting the gushing praise people gave me about Eve because I was always so overwhelmed by their genuine emotions. I knew Lisa liked me, but understanding she cared about me and my well-being was an entirely different thing.

"Finally, the slacker is back!" Greg said loudly and obnoxiously. "How dare you leave me like that!"

"The building is still standing, so I'm pretty sure you managed," I joked as we clapped each other on the back. "I just turned my phone back on and saw the number of messages. You're lucky I'm here at all. I almost threw my phone in the bay, grabbed Eve, and kept driving."

Greg laughed and started pushing me toward my office. "It's not that bad, I promise. You can delete most of them, it'll just take a few hours of your life to sift through them all."

I waved at Lisa and the others as we disappeared down the hallway. I flicked on the light to my office and was actually a little happy to see it. It was the same shade of gray Eve just painted our living room, which was surprisingly comforting. My desk was clear and my work bench still had my little projects right where I'd left them.

Ok, so being back at work wasn't nearly as horrible as I'd worked it up to be in my head.

Greg closed the door behind him and threw himself onto my couch. "Good honeymoon? You look good."

"Thanks," I replied as I set my bag down and sat at my desk. "It was perfect, actually. Almost didn't come home."

"I don't blame you. If I had a woman like Eve on a tropical island, I might not come back either."

I studied Greg trying to figure him out. He looked a little uncomfortable, which made me a little uncomfortable. "How were things here?"

"Smooth for the most part. You trained everyone really well. Only had a couple of hiccups."

Greg continued to fidget and he wasn't looking me in the eye which could only mean one thing. Something hadn't gone well with Ashley.

"How are things with The Nugget?"

Greg leaned forward and cracked his neck, "Not as well as I wanted. I was hoping to have everything taken care of by now. There are only a few loose ends but... Ashley's up to something, I think."

"You always think she's up to something."

He glared at me. "She *is* always up to something."

"Ok, let's get to the point. Where are we at?" I

didn't want to get into a fight with Greg in my first hour back at work.

"Steele is doing due diligence. Ash has been meeting with them for the last couple of days and you have meetings scheduled with them for the rest of the week. If everything goes as planned, the contracts will be ready on Monday."

That sounded great to me. "What's the catch?"

Greg shrugged, "Nothing, really. Something just feels off. I almost called and told you to take another week, but Steele wanted to meet with you personally. Fuckers."

"I can handle it. In fact, I'm kind of excited to put all of this to rest and move on with everything."

Greg looked at me like I was crazy. "Whatever you say."

There was a knock on my door and a second later Ashley poked her head inside uninvited. "Hey, I heard you were back."

"Come in," I replied, not really wanting her to come in.

She slid inside and closed the door. Greg glared at her so she stayed where she was, throwing an equally icy stare back at him. Clearly nothing had changed in my absence.

"So, Greg has been bringing me up to speed. We're on track for Monday?"

She smiled, "Yes. You sure you don't want to reconsider? Greg doesn't need you here, you know."

Greg rolled his eyes.

"Ash," I replied. "I'm very happy with where I'm

at. I like working with this big idiot."

"Hey," Greg scoffed. "This big idiot held down the fort while you took a vacation. Be nice to me."

"And I'm very grateful. We had a perfect honeymoon."

"Well," Ashley interrupted, "now that the dream is over and reality is back, I hope it's everything you're looking for."

I must have been feeling particularly fresh and confident because the next things out of my mouth were probably some of the dumbest things I'd ever said in all my life. "It will be. In fact, let's have a celebratory dinner at our house tomorrow night. Everyone can make nice and part on good terms." I wanted Eve to see for herself how little Ashley and I had between us, and I could make it clear to Ashley that this was the end of everything. It would be a perfect, clean break for everyone.

"Wonderful," Ashley said with a smile. She opened the door, "Let me know if you need me to bring anything." Then she left.

"You're an idiot." Greg sighed, standing up. "And I know exactly how this conversation goes from here so I'm going to save my breath and blood pressure. Check your calendar, everything is in there. Let me know if you have any questions."

He slammed the door behind him and I knew in the pit of my stomach I was going to regret being a moron.

Chapter 25

~Eve~

Jake, Greg, and Ashley were up in Jake's office going over the contracts while I was downstairs with Jennie and Andrew getting dinner ready.

"So that's her…" Andrew drawled with a sideways glance as he mixed a pitcher of mojito's. I was gonna need a nice tall glass of that. Or two. Hell, I wanted the whole damn pitcher. Having *her* in my house, laughing and existing… I just wanted to float away on a cloud of drunkeness.

"Yep."

Andrew cocked an eyebrow. "You like her that much, eh?"

I nodded as I finished chopping the last of the tomatoes. I was a notorious finger slicer when it came to prepping vegetables so I had to get it done before I got my greedy little hands on that first mojito.

"You're doing great. I'm pretty sure we'd all feel the same way in this situation."

I dumped the last of the diced tomatoes onto the avocado and onion mix already in the bowl. "There you go master chef. Turn that baby into guacamole."

"Not gonna talk to me about this?"

I smiled sweetly, "Not if you want the roof to stay on this house."

"Ouch. Ok..."

I didn't waste any time pulling out a tumbler, filling it with ice, and pouring a nice tall glass. The taste was sweet and bitter as it hit my tongue and the mint aftertaste was refreshing. It was exactly what I needed to stay happy around *her*.

Jake had been pretty cryptic about the whole dinner thing, but the vibe I got off of him was weird. I knew he wasn't telling me everything, but I also couldn't find a single bad intention anywhere in his behavior. I got the distinct impression he really needed this night.

Why—I had no idea. But considering how many things I still didn't understand about Jake's past, I decided to take a leap of faith in my new husband and hope to hell he knew what he was doing.

With every sip my shoulders got a little lighter and my fake smile got a little happier, until the entire kitchen seemed to lighten up.

I would make it through the night with the help of my good friend alcohol.

Jennie walked in and stared at me. I could only

imagine what I looked like leaned up against the counter with this ridiculous grin on my face. She shot Andrew a questioning look and he shrugged, "She's self-medicating. I decided it was probably a good idea."

It was a damn fine idea. Andrew and I had become excellent friends, and that was often strengthened by our silent understanding of each other.

Jennie cocked an eyebrow and rolled her eyes. "Whatever." Then she pulled me onto the porch where the grill was hot and ready for the steak we'd prepared for dinner. I plopped onto the lounge chair closest to the grill while Jennie busied herself with arranging the tongs and food. "Talk."

"Nope." I was sticking with single word answers. They were concise and effective.

"Yes." Jennie countered. "Now."

I stuck my tongue out at her and shrugged my shoulders. "Miserable."

"I would be, too." She let me be for a minute while she arranged the first round of steaks on the grill, then shut the lid and sat down beside me. "Has Jake lost his mind?"

I snort-laughed, it was very unlike me. "I'm wondering that myself."

"When you called to invite us over, I thought you were joking."

I took a deep breath and tried to focus through the mojito fog. "He's determined and I think that in his mind, tonight is proving some kind of point."

"That he's insane?" Jennie asked slowly.

"That he's not his past."

Jennie's eyes softened. "Oh. *Crap*."

"I know. I just couldn't get mad over it. He's clearly fighting Ashley and his past whether he realizes it or not. And he doesn't want to talk about it... or maybe *I* didn't want to talk about it. We just got home... things are supposed to be perfect for a while, aren't they?"

Jennie rubbed my arm and stood back up to check the steaks. "It's just dinner. If Jake needs this, then we'll all get through this together, for Jake."

"I don't trust her." I confessed.

"I don't blame you. I don't either."

Her camaraderie made me feel a little better. "My instincts tell me there is more to her than meets the eye. I trust Jake. I know he loves me and he'd never hurt me like that. But *her*... that is another story. I can't explain it. I just have a bad vibe."

Jennie glanced down at me. "Slow down on the alcohol. We don't want a scene."

***

We seriously have the best friends. They kept Ashley distracted for most of the dinner. Unfortunately the more I learned about her, the more human she became to me. I think Greg was catching on to that fact because he suddenly turned into Greg the Storyteller. He commanded the rest of the dinner with one hilarious story after another.

"And then Jake starts yelling at the bartender in German, which just totally confused the moron since we were in *England*, and instead of throwing us out, he poured us each a pint of Guinness and told us we needed to chill the fuck out."

Jake hung his head while he laughed quietly. His cheeks were a little red with embarrassment and it was kind of adorable. "Ok, ok... stop now before you tell them my real secrets!"

Greg grinned and his eyes were positively mischievous. "Oh, trust me, I'm saving those. It's always good to have ammunition."

Jake shook his head and grinned back. Oh, there was so much between those two I still had to learn. "Can I say something serious?" Jake asked looking around the table. "Good. First I want to thank all of you for coming over tonight. I really want to celebrate the selling of The Nugget and wish my friend Ashley well with her new opportunities at Steele Industries. I know she's going to set them on fire."

Ashley blushed and basked under Jake's praise.

I wanted to vomit.

"Thank you Jake." She had one of those soft, feminine voices that made my skin crawl.

Greg rolled his eyes while Jennie and Andrew both smiled politely.

"I'm sure," she continued with the oddest smile on her face, "That you'll do just fine here as well."

I thought it was a really strange statement and I was glad to see an equally confused look on Greg's face, but Jake seemed to simply brush it aside. He smiled and raised his glass before finishing off his whiskey.

I studied her as we all finished off our dinners. She was dressed in a simple blue dress that complimented her eyes and skin. Her red hair was smoothly styled over one shoulder and her makeup was perfect. She was flawless.

It was her lack of imperfections that really struck me. No one was that perfect.

Her smiles were so practiced and her laugh never quite seemed genuine. Everything about her looked perfect and sweet, but just beneath the surface there was a hint of something else. I just wasn't sure what.

I pushed back my chair and started gathering plates. Jake hopped up and grabbed the garbage can, helping me clear the table. He moved closer and closer until he was right behind me. I could feel his warmth a moment before he pressed into me.

All the tension I'd been fighting melted away and I took a deep breath. It was amazing how Jake could relax me just by touching me. Maybe I could forgive him for inviting her over to dinner.

Maybe.

It was really unlike him to ask something like this from me, so whatever was driving his need to have her over for dinner was obviously deep-seated. And that kind of scared me.

Jake knew I couldn't stand her.

He placed his hand lightly on my hip and nibbled at my earlobe before whispering in my ear, "I can't wait to kick all these people out of our house so I can have my way with you."

I turned my head so that I could look at him and whispered back, "That makes two of us."

Jake's eyes sparkled and he squeezed my hip before winking and moving around me to finish clearing the garbage.

I was dumbfounded. This Jake was a complete mystery to me.

"Can I get that for you?" Greg asked, holding out his hands for the last of the dishes.

"Sure," I replied.

He followed me into the kitchen, setting the stack on the sink. "So... tonight sucks."

I laughed. "Yep. Sure does."

"You doing ok?" He was genuinely concerned. His blue eyes were full of empathy.

"I am," I replied. "I'm just confused."

He huffed. "That makes two of us."

"Well crap. If you don't know what's going on with him and *I* don't know what's going on with him..."

Greg shook his head and leaned back against the counter with his arms crossed over his broad chest. "He never knew how to handle her and this is his way of proving a point."

"A point?" I asked.

"Yeah," he pulled me into a brotherly bear hug. "I think our boy is trying to send Ashley off into the sunset with the visual of him happy here. He thinks it will get through her head."

"You don't?" I didn't like the way Greg had said "thinks".

He sighed. "I honestly don't know. It just worries me."

"What are we going to do with my sweet, blind husband?"

Greg chuckled and gave me a squeeze before letting me go. "Let him work through this on his own and get his back like we always do."

"Thanks for being his friend." I didn't have the proper words in that moment to adequately tell Greg how much I loved having him as part of our family.

Greg stopped moving and simply nodded. He opened his mouth to reply but stopped when Jennie pranced in. "Let's get these dishes clean so we can have some fun!"

Jake had disappeared with Andrew to show him his latest cigar purchase while Jennie and Greg tackled the dishwasher, so I wandered into my library to escape all the weirdness I was feeling. The moment I was through the door I felt more at peace. This was my sanctuary. It was a place where all I had to do was pull a book—any book—off the shelf and I could escape into another world for a few minutes. I ran my hands along the book spines not really looking at the titles. I wasn't looking for something to read, just a momentary connection to that feeling of escape.

That was when *she* walked in. It was taking everything I had to not yell at her. Because I really just wanted to scream, "*Get out!*" but I was pretty sure it wouldn't go over so well on Miss Sweet and Delicate.

She stepped inside with confidence, but seemed to suddenly second guess her decision and shrink back, but it was too late to leave. Her blue eyes narrowed and she forced a smile onto her porcelain face.

For just a moment I daydreamed about using her face for pitching practice.

"Can I help you?" I tried to say it nicely, but it didn't quite come across that way. I really wanted her out of my house, out of my life, and out of my marriage.

To her credit, she didn't flinch or waver in any way. "Everyone seems to have disappeared." I wasn't buying her sweet and delicate routine for a minute.

"Jake and Andrew are upstairs, Greg is probably smoking on the porch, and who knows where the hell Jennie went."

"Jennie used to live here with you?"

Her question irritated me. "Yes, off and on since college. Sometimes she forgets this isn't her house anymore and disappears. She's probably freaking out because we redid the house after the wedding."

Ashley nodded as if that was an acceptable answer. "This room is beautiful." She walked over to the brown leather couch and ran her hands over the top cushion, which only irritated me more.

"Jake has his office, I have a library."

"You've read all these books?"

I shook my head, "No, I collect them. I like

knowing there is always something new to find."

Then she wandered over to the window that looked out over the backyard. "It is very peaceful here."

For the life of me I couldn't figure out why we were having a conversation. "Can we stop with the pleasantries and talk honestly for a minute?"

She spun to face me, her face a complete blank. I wished I could read her, maybe then I'd be able to understand the things I was feeling about her. I desperately wanted to know if it was my own fears coming through, or something I really needed to worry about.

Jake's bizarre behavior was throwing off my usual radar and I was really confused by all the extreme things I was feeling.

"I think that would be good for both of us. Eve, I'm honestly here for business and nothing else."

There were a thousand unspoken meanings to her words and I heard them all. It was in the cadence of her words and the rise and fall of her voice. I had no doubt in my mind she came here hoping to rekindle her relationship with Jake. Her disappointment was palpable and her conviction was thin at best—she was saying she had no interest in Jake to convince herself as much as me.

This was no time to doubt my instincts. If I had a bad feeling about her, then I needed to trust myself.

"I *honestly* find that hard to believe."

She blinked a couple of times, but didn't move. "*You* have always infatuated him, he came back for *you*, he married *you*. I'm fairly certain I lost this war before it even started, Eve."

I tried not to smile. It took everything I had. "And yet, I get the feeling that doesn't stop you."

"I think you and I are a lot alike in that department. We both go after what we want and we don't take no for an answer."

What was it about her that Jake found appealing?

He claimed it was nothing more than a friendship with obvious benefits, but it had to be more than that. Ashley was awful. I couldn't imagine Jake putting up with *her* for five years.

Sure she was freakishly beautiful, but this was Jake we were talking about. Even he wasn't that superficial.

"Are you still in love with him?"

I'd never seen someone with such a freakish ability to act, but Ashley was amazing. If I hadn't been looking her in the eyes when I asked my question I would have missed the two second flicker of passion she quickly extinguished.

"I loved him and we were good together."

Hearing another woman say she loved Jake—that they had something unique—probably hurt as much as Jake leaving me in the first place.

No, that was a lie. This hurt a helluva lot more.

"Greg seems to think you were the exact opposite of good for Jake." I whispered. I really, really wished she wasn't affecting me so much.

"I think that is a matter of perspective. Greg is a self-righteous ass. He had no idea what was really happening in Jake's life."

"But you know? You know better than any of the rest of us, am I right?"

"Exactly," she said quickly. "And I understand. Can you honestly say you will ever be able to understand how he feels or what he went through?" She waved her hands around my library. "You've had your whole life handed to you. You and Jake may as well have come from different planets."

The insult cut deep. "I think you have the wrong idea about me Ashley. I work very hard and very passionately for the life I want. If you think I'm a silly girl who just wants a pretty man to do my bidding then you've got another thing coming. I *love* Jake and I always have."

Ashley studied me for a long moment. "Jake only lets people see what he wants them to see. If you think you can understand him and be there for him in the way he really needs, well then *you've* got another thing coming." She took a step towards me. "And it will destroy you both."

Neither of us said a thing after that. The silence between us was cold and nearly tangible it was so thick with meaning.

"I'm going to say this once and only once," I was so angry I had to speak through my teeth. This other woman had come into my home and had the balls to tell me she still loved Jake and knew things about him no one else knew.

"*Stay away from my husband.* You have one opportunity." I held up my finger for emphasis.

"One. I do not give second chances. One slip up and I will have you tossed out of here so fast your head will spin. Trust me on that."

She took a defensive stance across from me. Miss Sweet and Delicate most definitely had a harder side. Her voice dropped, "I care about him, you know. I want him to be happy. He thinks he's safe with you, but I don't agree. I think he's in danger."

"In danger of what?" I was shocked, angry, and losing all my control.

"He has a fantasy in his head and when he realizes it's *just* a fantasy, he will be lost. Do you know what people like us look like when we're lost?"

"I do," I replied quietly. Her eyes sharpened for a moment—she didn't believe me. I imagined in her world, where I was a silly girl in love with the fantasy of Jake, I didn't have time to really get to know him, but she was wrong. I was there for him even when he tried to push me away. I saw first-hand what Jake looked like when he was lost and confused by the dueling thoughts in his head. "Let's get one thing clear, *Ashley*." Oh, how I hated saying her name, "There is one thing I care about more than anything else, and that's Jake. I can handle him, and anything else that comes our way, just fine. *I'm his wife*. I do not play games with the things I care about and I will do anything and everything to protect that."

Jake was the one thing in my life I would never compromise on.

"Make sure of it," she said. Then she turned toward the door to leave.

"Ashley, I mean it. One toe out of line and you'll wish you'd never set foot back in the States."

She glanced back at me over her shoulder, her eyes locking onto mine for just a moment. Then she nodded and left.

Chapter 26
-Jake-

If I plugged one more variable into one more formula I was going to lose my shit. I could not, for some reason, find the perfect balance between cost and safety that I wanted.

So I pushed back from the computer and decided what I needed was some time with my hands. In the corner of my office workshop was my pet project: a new robotic motor.

Working problems through with my hands was always the best way to relax my mind.

Well that, or working *Eve* over with my hands.

A shit-eatin' grin crept across my face as a dozen ideas for what to do when I got home flashed through my brain.

Yes, I liked working with my hands...

"Stop daydreamin' buttercup." Greg burst in through my main office door and threw himself on the couch by the door.

"I'm not daydreaming. I'm thinking."

"Tit, tat. Shit, shat. Whatever."

I set down the motor and turned toward Greg. "You have a gift for words, you know that, right?"

He grumbled and loosened his tie. "Look, I've just spent two hours in a meeting with Pita."

"Pita" was Greg-slang for Ashley. He called her the giant "Pain In the Ass". "What is with you two? I have never heard so many nicknames for one person."

Greg grinned, "The Annihilator and me, you mean? What does she call Pita?"

I rolled my eyes because the last thing I wanted to do was encourage either one of them. "Mostly she refuses to refer to Ashley by name. She calls her, *her*. But her other nickname is Miss Sweet and Delicate."

Greg snorted. "I like it. The sarcasm is perfect."

"You two should really cool it. Ash doesn't deserve it."

Greg raised his eyebrows and huffed. "You are an idiot, my friend. A blind, stupid idiot."

Greg had never liked Ashley. Not ever. I usually just chalked it up to their extremely different personalities. Sometimes women and men just don't get along.

Ashley was definitely the kind of woman who liked to be treated like a woman. She wanted manners and preferential treatment at all times. She always acted the part of the Sweet and Delicate flower. Greg, on the other hand, despised being required to treat women so carefully. It was his belief there was a time and place for that kind of behavior. And it was not at work.

"Why am I a blind, stupid idiot?" I sighed.

He just shook his head like I was some poor sap. "She isn't who you think she is. She's had you wrapped around her pretty little finger since day one. You liked it back then. Fuck, maybe it was even what you needed. Hell if I know. All I know is she is as fake as they come. She is one giant act. Your wife deserves an Academy Award for living through last night."

"What now?"

"Oh, come on," Greg threw his hands in the air. "She hates Ashley, and yet she smiled all night long. Sure, she was half drunk at dinner, but really, I couldn't blame her for that. You sir, are an asshole."

My defenses shot up faster than Greg's words could sink in. "This is none of your damn business, Greg."

That was when I knew I was in trouble. Greg seared a hole through me with a stare that made my blood run cold. I'd seen him mad before, and what I was looking at now was on an entirely different level. When he spoke, his voice was quiet and controlled. "What happens between you and Eve is your business, but when you hurt her, you are messing with me, too."

"You are *my* friend, not hers." I don't even know why I said that. It was so far off point.

Greg let out a long slow breath and the vein in his

neck throbbed. "Let's get one thing straight: I am friends with *both* of you. But if I had to pick a side right now, it would be hers."

"How did I hurt her?" I was being entirely too defensive, but I couldn't stop myself. "She said she was fine with Ashley."

Greg looked at me like I was a child. "Eve was fine with giving you what you asked for because she loves you, you big dumb asshole. It does not mean she was fine with having your ex-lover under her roof. Are you telling me if Eve asked Sebastian over to work out a few lingering issues from their past you wouldn't be upset and wondering what the hell was happening to your marriage?"

Just the mention of Eve's ex-boyfriend made me want to punch a hole in the wall. It didn't matter that she didn't love him. I hated everything about that man and spending one party in the same room with him was as much as I could tolerate for one lifetime. "I thought Eve was better than me," I said as much to myself as to Greg.

He rolled his eyes. "She is."

That hurt, but it was true.

I sat there quietly because I didn't know what to say. I had totally and completely misread Eve. Greg was right—I an idiot. "I honestly thought she was simply better at putting the past away than I was."

"The past, maybe. Your old flame? Eve? Really? Seriously," he shook his head at me, "when you're getting relationship advice from *me,* you're in a bad place my friend."

"Shit." I couldn't sit still. I wanted fix things with Eve right then and there.

Greg laughed at me as he stood up and headed toward the door. "If I were forced to have dinner with my wife's ex-lover, I probably would have gotten even drunker than Eve, then ripped out the assholes esophagus and beaten him to death with it. She must really love your loser ass."

Greg could seriously paint a mental picture like no one else. "You don't have a wife."

"And it's a damn good thing, too."

I stopped on my way home and bought Eve's favorite chocolate cake from the little French bakery she loved. We'd been home less than a week and I'd already screwed everything up. If I was lucky she wouldn't divorce me. I really didn't know how to make up for last night. I'd never really had to make up with Eve before. Not like this.

When I opened the front door I was hit on all fronts. Music was blaring, food was obviously cooking, and lights were low with candles lit everywhere. I found Eve singing and dancing in the kitchen, her back to me, while she chopped vegetables. I didn't want to scare her with a knife in her hands, so I dangled the bag with the cake from my index finger and cleared my throat loudly.

She spun around and grinned at me, her eyes dropping to the bag and back up again. "Hey there. What have we here?"

She was wearing a tank top and exercise shorts— and obviously nothing else. I was instantly turned on. "I brought you dessert."

Her eyes flashed with something dark and dirty. Dessert was rarely eaten with a fork in our house. "To what do I owe such a lovely surprise?" She took a step toward me, taking the bag and placing it on the counter.

She was inches away, and yet I could feel her body warmth. I wanted to touch her, but I held back. "I wanted to apologize for last night."

Her eyes flicked up to mine, but she didn't say a word. Her breathing changed, but it wasn't heavy with desire like I'd hoped. It was ragged, like she was upset. "Oh," she finally said. Then she leaned back against the counter, crossing her arms protectively across her chest. "How was work today?"

I wanted to pull her into my arms, rip the barrier between us away, and physically force her to forgive me, but I knew that wasn't going to work. I couldn't fix my screw-up with a hug or sex. I needed to start talking. "Work was fine. Normal." I explained. "Greg took the meetings with Ashley and I didn't see her at all."

I honestly couldn't read Eve. She was stone—no expression on her face anywhere. "And I wanted to say thank you. I needed last night but I know it must have been hard for you."

She blinked a few hundred times. "Hard?" she finally said. "Hard? You invite your ex over and you think it was *hard* for me? You are such a fucking hypocrite!"

Yeah, that hurt a little. "I know I asked things of

you I couldn't do myself. But I really needed to close that chapter."

Eve looked like she wanted to punch me as she turned away and paced around the kitchen. "Do you realize you didn't even ask me how I was last night?" She stopped and glared at me from across the island. "When they left, you just asked me if I was ready for bed, we had quick sex, and turned out the lights." She threw her hands up in the air and looked at the ceiling. "I had dinner with your ex and all you had in you was quick sex and a cuddle?"

She was almost yelling by that point and I couldn't blame her. "I was a selfish asshole, Eve."

She balled up her fists and screamed at me. It was unintelligible, but clearly full of curse words. "Are you fucking kidding me?"

I took my life into my own hands and calmly walked around the island, placing my hands on her hips. "I needed her to see that I have a good life here. One she could never be a part of. That my old life is dead and gone, and my new life is the best thing that has ever happened to me. Ash is a visual person. I could tell her until I was blue in the face that I loved my company and being married to you was exactly what I needed, but until she could see it for herself, it wasn't going to sink in."

I expected Eve to soften, to allow me to kiss her or hold her, but that wasn't what happened. She put her palms on my chest and pushed me away instead. "Ashley and I had a very interesting conversation after dinner, Jake. One in which she told me how much she loved you."

Well that was an interesting development. A really unexpected, crappy, development.

I was in much deeper shit than I realized.

Eve paced around to the opposite side of the island, crossed her arms back over her chest, and glared at me. "I'm not sure your grand plan worked, Jake."

"What did you say to her?" I asked tentatively.

The corners of her lips twitched up in an evil smile. One I kind of found a little hot. "I did what I do. I warned her she wouldn't like stepping on my territory."

I felt my own lips twitch up a little. "I love you."

"I know. But you're still a selfish bastard."

"I should have talked this over with you first, huh?"

She shook her head and rolled her eyes. "Jake, I know you're still getting used to having a wife and not simply making blanket decisions for yourself... but yeah, this is one of those things you should have cleared with me first."

I took a chance and started to slowly walk around the island. It felt like Eve was warming up to me. Possibly even willing to forgive me. "I'm sorry. I thought I was doing the right thing."

She sighed and closed her eyes. "I don't understand, Jake. I feel like you're keeping things from me."

Part of me wanted to tell Eve everything, I always wanted to tell her everything, but with Ashley it was different. Telling Eve everything would only make things more confusing and it wasn't my story to tell. "I'm not going to lie to you, Eve. I'm going to be brutally honest and I'll let you decide what you what to know. Ok?"

I dipped down to catch her gaze. It was such a relief to look into her eyes. Sure she was as mad as ever, but what I really saw was confusion. "Start talking, Jake. My patience isn't going to last forever."

"Alright. I've told you just about everything there is to know about my relationship with her, so if you are worried about that, don't be. It was exactly what I told you—a convenient friendship."

I felt Eve tense under my hands and she was looking at my chest, not my eyes, but she was listening.

"I never loved her. Hell," I sighed, "I wasn't even a very good friend. I was very selfish and wasn't in a place to really care about anyone. She knew that and she knew what she was getting herself into, so I always absolved myself of any blame when it came to our past. That was probably shitty of me, too."

Damn, I was such a horrible person. The more I heard myself talk, the more I hated myself. So many mistakes...

"I hate that you know so much about my past, and I can't change it. But Ashley's..." I swallowed and looked up at Eve. She was staring at me with her arms wrapped around her body.

"How bad is it?" her voice was so quiet.

"Bad," was all I said. But it was all I needed to say.

Eve nodded once and started rubbing her arms like
she was cold. I wanted to walk over to her and make
her warm, but I gave her a second to process
everything I was saying instead.

"And you don't want to tell me about it?"

I shook my head. It was the last thing I wanted. I
didn't like knowing Ashley's history, how could
anyone else? "No. I don't want to put someone else's
shitty history in your lap. I just want to leave the
damn past in the past already."

I could feel every inch of the distance between us
and I hated all of it. "I'm trying to understand," she
finally said.

"I'm sorry I invited her over here and I'm even
more sorry I didn't stop to think how all of this might
affect you. I don't know what the hell is wrong with
me." I really didn't.

Eve sighed and shook her head, then she crossed
the kitchen and came to stand right in front of me.
"There is nothing wrong with you, Jake. You're in a
weird situation and you're trying to do the right
thing. I get that. But..."

I raised my eyebrows, "But?"

"But you have to talk to me. You can't just assume
you know what I'm thinking or what is best for me."

"I'm sorry," I repeated. "It was a dickhead move
to do all of this without talking it through with you
first." I genuinely felt like a moron.

"The thing is," she smiled up at me, "it's one of the
things I really find very hot most of the time. I like
decisive, commanding Jake. So I guess I have to

accept a few misses here and there."

"You like the cocky bastard routine, don't you Eve?" All the distance between us was vanishing. She was letting me back in.

Her chest was rising and falling rapidly. "I love cocky Jake. Yes."

I picked her up and set her down on the counter in front of me, pushing her knees out so I could settle between her thighs. Eve rested her hands gently on my shoulders. She didn't pull me against her, but she didn't push me away either.

I ran my nose up her throat and settled behind her ear. She shivered.

"Forgive me?"

Her hands curled around my shoulders as she sucked in an excited breath, but Eve still didn't answer me.

So I ran my right hand up her thigh and pressed my thumb up against her sex at the exact moment I whispered in her ear, "Please forgive me, Eve."

She whimpered and nodded. "I forgive you."

Then I tugged on her earlobe while I moved my thumb under her shorts, finding the warm, wet promise of make-up sex. "I love you so much."

"I love you, too," she groaned, running her fingers up into my hair and pressing my lips against her chest.

I grinned. Having my face planted between her breasts with my hand up her shorts was probably one of the best places in the world. "How can I make it up to you?"

I pressed my thumb inside her and she arched her back, groaning and pulling me against her with her feet. "Shut up, you cocky bastard. You know what I want."

Chapter 27
~*Eve*~

Jake pushed inside me with his thumb and I forgot everything we were talking about. How could I think about the past or my anger when his thumb was doing fantastic things to the most sensitive part of my body?

He pulled me closer to the edge of the counter and I leaned back on my hands. I was so turned on I couldn't see straight, so I closed my eyes and enjoyed the way Jake was saying he was sorry. "Don't be quiet. I want to hear everything you're feeling," his voice was hoarse.

But it was more than that. He was looking for a way into my head through sex.

"I hate you for last night."

He groaned and kissed his way down my neck to my chest. When his mouth found my nipples under the thin fabric of my tank top I let him hear just how

253

aroused I was, too.

"Oh baby..." he sighed.

I grinned as I ran my fingers through his hair and his thumb turned into two fingers stroking and massaging until I was panting and tugging at his hair for leverage. "You didn't talk to me."

He pulled back and looked up into my eyes. "I won't make that mistake twice."

He kissed me with one hand in my hair and one inside my body and, for a minute, I forgot about everything but loving Jake. "She's not you," I whispered. I knew I was treading into territory I probably couldn't navigate, but I dove in anyway. Jake stilled, but didn't look up at me. I kept talking. "Jake, in any other world I would have had her tossed out on her backside and I probably would have picked a huge fight with you. But I couldn't. This is complicated and I know it. As much as I want this to be a black and white issue, it isn't." I grabbed his chin and tilted his face up to mine. "I know you're confused and I'm trying to be understanding, but you have to trust me."

He swallowed and the dark look in his eyes about broke my heart. "I trust you more than I've ever trusted anyone, Eve." He slowly pulled his fingers out of my body and wrapped himself around me, burying his face in my shoulder. "I do trust you. I just don't always know how to say what's going on in my head because I don't know what's going on in my head."

I wished holding him could actually make Jake's

problems go away. "But you're writing, right?"

He nodded against my shoulder, digging his fingers into my sides as he held me tighter. "Yes."

"Good. Keep writing and try to talk to me more, ok? We'll get through this."

He started kissing my neck and massaging my hips. He was upset and thinking too much about things he couldn't change. That was when my eyes fell on the bag he brought home. "I think we should eat dessert before dinner."

I felt his grin against my skin. "I think that is a fantastic idea."

While we ate dessert, dinner got cold. Not that I cared. Jake reenacted round two of our wedding night with shocking precision. Licking chocolate off of each other was one of my new favorite ways to relax.

The combination of memories and emotions was overwhelming.

He was on the counter on his back with me draped across his chest. I was exhausted and relaxed and oddly happy, all things considered. Words started falling out of my mouth before I could stop them. "When we're like this, I'm always happy. When it's just you and me... nothing else matters. It's everything else that gets in the way."

He was rubbing my back and pulling his fingers through my hair. The rise and fall of his broad chest was as comforting as anything I'd ever felt. "If I could find a way to hide us away, I would," he whispered.

I thought about our honeymoon and how happy we were for those two weeks. Why couldn't the rest of our lives be just as simple? "I think that should be our goal. You and me."

He was quiet for a minute and I wondered what he was thinking about but I still didn't want to push him. Jake needed to work through all of this himself. "We should really eat some dinner..." he chuckled.

It took a few minutes in the microwave to warm our food back up. We ate dinner cross legged on the counter. "How have we never done this before?" Jake asked as he shoved a forkful in his mouth.

"I don't know, but we can do it again any time. Especially if we have sex as an appetizer."

Jake grinned, his dimple showing in his left cheek.

I looked Jake in the eye. "You do realize that after this, if any other ex's or Miss Sweet and Delicate shows up again, I'm enacting a zero tolerance policy, right?"

"I had no doubt. Thank you for understanding that this was a unique situation."

I studied him while he ate. I still don't think he really understood. To him, Ashley was in the same position he'd been in once. She just needed someone to help. I could see his point of view—that turning his back on Ashley was like turning his back on himself. Jake was too close to his own situation. He couldn't see what Greg and I could see: he and Ashley weren't in the same position. Helping her and dragging us along for the ride wasn't going to fix things and it certainly wasn't going to redeem anyone.

Once is a lesson. Twice wasn't going to happen.

Chapter 28
-Jake-

I was sitting in yet another conference room waiting for yet another meeting... with Ashley... when all I really wanted was to be with Eve, who was also stuck in a late meeting at work. I hoped to hell after everything was settled on Monday our lives would get a lot simpler. A week ago we were relaxing and having sex. This week we were stressed and busy. I didn't like this change at all.

It felt late, my sense of time was still all off from our honeymoon, so I was surprised when I glanced at my watch and saw it *was* late. I had just grabbed my phone when Ashley walked in.

"Sorry, I forgot to tell you. They cancelled the meeting and pushed everything until tomorrow. I think if we are concise we'll still manage to get it all in."

This was not good news. Hiccups were never good

news. "Any particular reason? Should we be worried?"

She shook her head, her long red waves dancing back and forth. "No, just something came up that required their attention. It has nothing to do with us. But..."

I raised an eyebrow. I really didn't like where this was going now. "But?"

"It is a perfect opportunity for you and me to finalize everything."

Alarm bells went off in my head. There was no reason to "finalize" anything. Besides, I had an entire company that could use my attention. "I don't think so."

She leaned against the conference table and rolled her eyes. "Despite what your wife thinks, I don't actually bite."

"That would be Greg. *Greg* thinks you bite. Eve just thinks you shoot lasers out of your eyes."

She chuckled and looked down at her hands. "I understand all of this is bad timing, but it has been nice to see you again, Jake. I really do miss our friendship."

It was times like this I simply couldn't tell what Ashley was really saying. I honestly thought she was being real. But according to Greg and Eve, she was one big act. Was this real or an act?

Why couldn't I tell the difference?

Having that doubt was something I hated feeling. It brought up old and very deep-seated issues about trusting myself. "People change and move on. It's life, Ash."

She looked me in the eye. "I still can't believe you are signing away your rights. Does she hate me that much?"

That floored me. "It wasn't her choice. It was mine."

"All these years... she must really be something special. I don't think I believed you until now. I always thought she was either a figment of your imagination or you were so in love you didn't see her for who she was."

I hated every single thing Ashley had just said. It was a serious reaction. Anger immediately boiled up inside me. Ashley could say whatever she wanted to about me, or even Greg, but Eve was off-limits. "Then you must not have ever really known me."

She blinked and a look of complete surprise washed over her face. "Maybe. But I like to think I know you in a way no one else ever will."

That stung as much as the other things she'd said. "What the hell is that supposed to mean?"

"Why do you think you and I worked?" she asked, standing up and glaring at me. "I'm the only one in your life who really understands your dark places because I have the same ones. Greg doesn't understand your doubts and Eve doesn't understand your darkness. Not like I do. *I* understand you. And if you think you are better off with Greg and Eve than you are with me, then fine. But just keep in mind— *they don't know you like I do.*"

"You must have a nice fantasy life because I sure

as hell don't remember our relationship the same way you do."

She took another step toward me. I didn't like that she was standing while I was sitting. The power dynamic felt all wrong. "When you doubt yourself, you get jumpy because you're looking for the closest exit. When you do something wrong, you beat yourself up inside just as bad as your dad would beat you up on the outside. And when you're alone, you know you are never going to be good enough for anyone else."

I didn't reply to her. Not right away. If I had, I would have said a lot of really terrible things. Things I never would have forgiven myself for. So instead, I stood up slowly, adjusted my tie, and took a deep breath before looking Ashley in the eyes.

"You are right about every single one of those things." I hated that she was right. "But that doesn't mean you know me. I am so much more than what that man trained me to be. And I'll be damned if I let you or anyone else tell me I have to stay that way."

She studied me for a minute and it took all of my self-restraint to keep from throwing her out of the conference room by her hair. "You should be with someone who understands you, not someone who will get your hopes up and watch you fall when you can't live up to her expectations. You are setting yourself up for misery, Jake."

"I think we're done here."

She chuckled a little, "You'll know where to find me when she crushes you under her boot. I'll be waiting, Jake."

"That will be a cold day in hell."

She shrugged her shoulders and then stalked out of the room.

***

When I got home, my bedroom was empty. Hell, my whole house was empty. And even worse... Eve wasn't answering her phone. I was in full panic mode. She should have been home at least an hour ago.

I'd done it all: flowers, dinner, wine, and a new movie.

But my guest of honor was missing and I was in a dark, confusing place.

As much as I hated to admit it, Ashley had done a number on me. She'd hit every button and played on every insecurity I had. I needed to screw my head back on straight.

I needed Eve.

"Jake?" her voice rang through the empty house.

"In here," I called.

I'd given myself quite the lecture. I was going to give her time to explain why she was late. I was going to be understanding.

"You're home early... and sitting in the dark with a drink? What happened?"

She set her bag down on the counter and peeled off her blazer. It was funny how simple her outfit looked this morning, but now it seemed sexy. Damn sexy. Her top was unbuttoned to her breasts. Her *perfect* breasts. My sun necklace only drew my attention to them even more. Her pants clung to her curves accentuating her amazingly sexy body.

Why did she have to look so hot in everything she wore?

"How long have you been sitting here?"

I glanced down at my watch, "An hour. You didn't answer your phone."

Her eyes widened some more and she flipped her bag open, "I've had it on silent since my meeting started. I'm so sorry."

"You didn't answer your office phone either."

She set her phone quietly on the counter and spun toward me. "Jake, stop. Whatever you're thinking... just stop."

"Eve, you *always* answer your phone. Always. What happened tonight?" I desperately wanted her to have a simple and easy explanation that would make all of these ridiculous worries in my male pea-brain go away.

She put her balled up fists on her hips and glared at me. "Please, tell me how your day with Miss Sweet and Delicate went."

"This is not about me, Eve. I came home *to an empty house*." She was not turning the tables on me.

"Then why aren't you answering me? Just because you came home on time doesn't mean nothing happened during *your* day."

"I have nothing to hide. Unlike you, who seem to be hell bent on keeping your missing hours a fucking secret!"

For a split second I saw fire in her eyes. "You have lost your mind!"

She spun on her heel and stomped out of the room, but there was no way I was letting her out of there while we were still talking. "Eve, get back in here. We are not done."

"Fuck off!" she yelled, stomping down the hallway.

"Hell no. You are my wife and we having this discussion whether you like it or not."

She slammed the library door in my face and turned the lock before I could get my hand on the handle. It didn't stop me from trying anyway. I was too pissed to be calm and reasonable. I jiggled the handle and beat my fist against the door. "Eve, open the damn door."

"Fuck. Off." she yelled back and I heard the squeaky sound of her throwing herself on the leather couch.

I hit the door again and then rested my forehead against the cool surface. I absolutely hated having a barrier of any kind between us. It felt physically wrong on a good day, but when we were fighting I wanted to incinerate anything that kept me from her.

The fact she wouldn't tell me what she was doing kept running through my head on a loop. "Eve, I'm serious. We need to talk."

"And I need to calm down. Go away, Jake."

Calm down? Calm down? What in the hell did she have to calm down from? She was the one who stayed late at work and didn't answer her phone. "If you don't open this door I will go full-on Rhett Butler. I will kick this door in and carry you up the stairs kicking and screaming." I'd been forced to watch that movie with Eve more times than I could count.

The lock clicked and the door opened. "You are such a bastard sometimes."

I let her walk back across the room while my anger boiled. "I may be a bastard, but I love you. There is nothing scarier than the idea of losing you. Maybe I'm an asshole and I'm overreacting, but I'm *your* asshole. I will overreact any time I damn well please when it comes to you."

Her arms were crossed and there was a scowl on her face, but the corners of her lips turned up just a little. "Where is this coming from?"

I suddenly realized I'd picked a fight with my wife on purpose. I was completely rattled by Ashley. "Ashley was weird today."

Eve flushed a little. Her blood pressure must have just skyrocketed up to my level. "Weird how?"

"Apparently she thinks she knows me better than anyone else ever has or ever could."

Eve shot up off the couch, marched right past me, and out of the library. "Where are you going?" I asked as she grabbed her keys from the bowl by the door.

"I'm gonna kill her!"

Eve was hot when she was mad. "Don't leave. You don't need to kill her."

She reached for the door handle just as I rushed forward and wrapped my arm around her waist, pulling her body back against mine. The contact mixed with her scent set my senses on fire.

"Let me go! I need to kick the crap out of her delicate ass!"

"No," I whispered against the sensitive part of her ear. "Don't leave me. I need you right now."

"Fuck," she sighed, relaxing back against me.

I took the keys from her hands and tossed them at the table (missing completely, I might add) while she pushed the door shut and locked it, keeping her palms flattened against the smooth surface.

"I want to rip out her throat."

I smiled against the skin of her neck and flexed my fingers into the soft flesh of her hips. "And that makes me love you even more."

She leaned forward, letting her head move down between her shoulders and her ass press against my quickly hardening cock.

When she spoke it was a whisper. I had absolutely no idea I was feeling so tested until that moment. "Does she?" I knew exactly what Eve meant, but I was too overwhelmed to respond. "Does she know a part of you I can't?"

I spun Eve to face me, pressing her back into the door as I moved against her with my hands and elbows flattened against the door beside her head and my body pressed flush against her.

"There are two people who know all my weaknesses and vulnerabilities, Eve. And both of them use it to their own advantage. Ashley knows how to exploit me, Eve. She's more screwed up than I was. Maybe she still is." I felt so raw. I'd been wrong about so many things.

There was one thing that mattered to me, and I was staring into her beautiful eyes. "You are my life." I kissed her gently on the lips. "After today, I hate Ashley almost as much as I hate my father. I didn't realize that until she tried to convince me I was better off being the man I *used* to be. She has no idea, Eve. She doesn't *me* at all. You do. You know me and everything I want to become. That difference is everything."

The two of us became something else entirely at that point. We were ruled by emotions and driven by desperation. Eve unbuttoned her own blouse, popping a couple of buttons along the way, while I unbelted her pants and pushed them down toward her ankles. A minute later I had her pressed up against the front door while I buried myself inside her.

I grunted while Eve moaned, pulling hard on my hair as I nailed her to the door with her legs wrapped around my waist. "Oh god, Jake. Harder..." she moaned. It was like she wanted me to brand her. As if how hard I was pumping into her was somehow comparable to how much need I had for her.

"Harder..." she moaned again.

The door wasn't going to cut it. I couldn't get the kind of leverage we needed. I spun us around and lowered her back onto the rug, driving deeper inside her. Her head fell back and her eyes rolled into her head. We both seemed to like the new angle.

I placed my elbows above her shoulders to keep from driving her across the floor and giving her rug burn. Eve pressed her heels into my bare ass, begging me to continue.

By the time she was screaming my name, her hair was a mess and I was sweaty and breathless. I collapsed on top of her, our muscles twitching and my cock spasming inside her while her body continued to randomly pulse around mine. These emotion-fueled sessions were more intense and exhausting than anything I'd ever done.

She was panting and her eyes were closed as I kissed up and down her neck. "I love you Eve."

She ruffled my hair and smiled with her eyes still closed. "Tell me she ever loved you like I do."

It was what I'd said to her about Sebastian. "No Eve. No one will ever love me like you."

Chapter 29
~Eve~

It was well after midnight. The moonlight was streaming in through the open blinds and bathing our bedroom in a blue-white glow. It threw long shadows across the floor and bed, and cast Jake's sleeping face in darkness. His bare chest and arms were exposed but the red blanket covered the rest of his body.

Maybe he was sexy as hell, or maybe it was just because he was Jake and I was Eve, but I loved his body. I always had. Young and lean Jake was every bit as handsome and sexy to me as grown-up and strong Jake. I loved running my hands over the hard lines of his muscles and feeling the deceptive softness of his skin beneath my fingers.

When I couldn't sleep, I always sat up and studied him. Like everything else concerning my husband, he was an example of extremes. He was either twisted and tortured as nightmares I couldn't imagine ruined his sleep, or more peaceful and relaxed than I'd ever seen him.

He didn't know it, but if I saw him having a nightmare I always woke him up. Sometimes I would pretend it was me, that I had just woken up from a nightmare and needed him to hold me. Other times I would simply nestle into the side of him and gently shake him until the nightmare subsided.

Tonight, miraculously, he was peaceful. So I was watching him sleep, wishing I felt even half as relaxed as he did.

I was frustrated.

No, fuck that. I was pissed. I had a barely contained anger burning inside me and I wasn't sure what to do with it. There was what I wanted to do, and what I knew I *should* do.

Jake wanted me to let the Ashley incident go, suffer through Monday, and let her ride off into the sunset—hopefully to never be heard from again.

But it didn't feel like enough. What Jake described to me tonight was unacceptable. One screwed up abuser in his life was too many, but two...

I didn't just want Ashley to leave, I wanted to destroy her.

And so there I was, sitting up in the middle of the night trying to make sense of my feelings. I thought about calling Jennie. I knew she'd talk to me, but I was too afraid she'd talk me down off the crazy ledge.

I liked it on the crazy ledge and I had no intentions of quietly climbing back down.

I'd hoped my initial threat would have worked, but clearly Miss Sweet and Delicate either didn't see me as a truly terrifying threat, or I was barking up the wrong tree.

I had a very good feeling I needed a new tree. I needed to find what made her tick and hit her where it hurt.

I unplugged my phone from the nightstand and slid out of our room. Inside my library I cuddled up on the couch and texted Greg.

A minute later my phone rang.

"Did I wake you?"

Greg snorted, "Do I sound asleep?"

No, actually he sounded wide awake. "Thanks for calling."

"No problem. Why are *you* awake?"

"I need to know more about Pita. I need to know what makes her tick."

"He told you my nickname? Do you like it?" he sounded like a giddy kid sharing a new secret.

"It's perfect. I'm a little sad I didn't think of it myself, actually. It's so much more concise than mine."

"But, yours is very accurate."

We were both quiet for a minute. "I tried, Greg. I really did."

"You tried harder than you needed to, in my opinion. What did she do?"

I debated how much to divulge. On the one hand, Greg was Jake's best friend. They told each other most things and I certainly didn't feel the need to keep things from him. But on the other hand, this was very personal and I wasn't sure Greg needed to know the particulars. I decided to play things close to the vest. Less information was usually better in my experience. "I gave her a line and she crossed it today."

There was grumble on the other end of the line. "That explains my afternoon. She was hell on wheels and Jake barely said two words when he left."

"I want to hurt her."

"I don't blame you." his voice was eerily low. I got the impression Greg was almost as mad as I was. I wondered if Jake knew how much he was loved— really loved—by the people in his life.

"And I need to make sure she gets the message loud and clear this time. There is no place for her here."

"Fuck yeah. Well, let me tell you what I know..."

Greg and I talked for the next thirty minutes. He clued me in on everything he knew about Ashley from the professional end: who her mentors were, where she attended school, what her plans were for the future.

One thing was clear. Ashley was more like Jake Sr. than I ever realized. Her red-headed beautiful exterior was window dressing on a monstrosity hiding inside. She was a wolf in sheep's clothing. She was evil.

And like all evil people, she thought she was in control. She thought she was playing her part perfectly, pulling the strings and watching the puppets dance.

She didn't know she was playing with fire.

I thought Ashley knew Jake in a way I couldn't.

I was wrong.

I *did* know that side of Jake, I just knew it from a completely different side. Ashley knew it from the side of controller.

I knew it from Jake's side.

She only thought she knew him. And Jake only wished I didn't know that part of him.

But I did.

I always knew that part of him. It was one of the most beautiful gifts of being in love with your soul mate: I didn't need to know every sordid detail, I didn't need to have lived the same life, or experienced the same pain. All I needed was to know Jake.

And I knew him better than anyone else.

I knew who Jake was the night we met. I looked into those expressive green eyes of his and saw all of him. The man I saw that night was the same man sleeping in our bed with my wedding ring on his finger. His heart and mine were the same. I felt his pain and doubt just as strongly as I felt my own.

I knew exactly how to deal with the demons in Jake's life. Ashley had made a grave mistake in assuming I wouldn't understand. The truth was, I understood her all too well.

I was going to annihilate her.

"Greg, I need your help."

Chapter 30
-Jake-

The moment I stepped foot into the office I knew something was wrong. There was a weird vibration to the air and Lisa didn't meet my eyes, let alone smile.

"Good morning, Jake."

"Morning, Lisa. What gives?"

She smiled tightly, but still didn't quite look at me. "Greg is in a closed door meeting with Ashley."

My eyebrows shot up, "Already? Is something wrong?"

She shrugged her shoulders slowly, "I'm not sure, but Greg was in one of his moods this morning."

"Good mood or bad mood?"

"We called him Hurricane Greg."

Bad mood. *Really* bad mood. "How long have they been in there?"

She fiddled with the papers beside her keyboard

before answering, "About thirty minutes. And..."

"And?" I asked expectantly.

"And he said to have you wait in your office."

I stalked right past her reception desk on a collision course with Greg's office door.

"Jake! No, he really doesn't want you in there!"

I ignored her, of course, and shoved the door open. Greg was leaned back in his chair with a devilish grin on his face and Ashley was sitting across from him with a completely blank expression on hers. "What's up guys? I'm sorry I'm late."

"Shut the fucking door if you insist on barging in."

I slammed the door shut and stood where I was with my arms crossed over my chest.

Ashley swung her gaze over to me and that was when I realized her blank look was deceiving. Her eyes were blazing. She was pissed.

"The deal with Steele Industries is falling through," Greg explained.

Whoa... Of all the things I expected to walk into, that wasn't it. "What happened? Why now?"

"Sugar Plum Fairy here made them jittery when she cancelled the meeting yesterday."

"You? *You* cancelled the meeting? You told me it was them."

The color drained from her face a little but she stayed silent. Greg continued, "They pulled the offer for Ashley to come work with them. They want to buy-out both of you outright, or they are walking."

You could have heard a pin drop in that office. "And you don't want to sell your stake, still." It was a statement. I knew the answer.

"If you changed your mind, I'm sure they'd reconsider. I made a stupid mistake letting my own issues get in the way of business, but at the end of the day, Steele wants our design and they want both of us on their team. I'm sure if you reconsider, we can still make this happen."

Ashley looked so stupidly earnest and Greg was grinning like a fool. He knew my answer was no. She should know my answer was no.

"Ash, I'm a partner in *this* firm. I have no interest in going to work for someone else, no matter what kind of innovative work they are doing. I like my life here. *This* is what I want."

She smiled up at me wanely. "I know, but it was worth a try. Is there anything I can do to sway you? We make a great team. Who knows what we might invent next?"

"I don't care. I like my work, but I love my life. *I love my wife.*" *I want to have a family and watch my kids grow up.*

The thought hit me like a lightning bolt from the sky. It was a revelation at the oddest of times, but even as the idea surged through my veins, I knew without a shadow of a doubt it was what I wanted.

She stood up and smoothed her skirt before tossing her red hair back over her shoulder. "Well, then it seems I have some thinking to do. And some phone calls to make."

The moment she was gone, I pushed the door closed again and took the chair she'd just vacated across from Greg. "What really happened?"

Greg's face didn't give anything away. He was a master poker player and his skills extended well beyond the game. "I have no idea what you are talking about. I was just as surprised as both of you when the phone call came in this morning."

"You had nothing to do with this?"

"Do with what?" he asked with a silly grin, floating his hands through the air like birds wings.

I shook my head and rolled my eyes. Greg may not have been the reason Steele pulled the offer at the last minute, but he sure helped push. I might not be able to read his poker face, but I knew the look of mischief and pride. Greg had both right now.

"Hopefully she finds another deal fast. I don't want her sticking around any longer."

"She won't find one she likes," he smirked.

"What do you mean? What did you do?"

"She's just getting what was coming to her. She had the upper hand on a fantastic opportunity and she blew it because she was greedy. She wanted more. The money and the job offer weren't enough—she wanted you, too. All I've done is answer some questions in a brutally honest way. It isn't my fault Steele took that as a sign Ashley might not be the employee they were looking for. It is also not my fault I passed that same information along to quite a few of my contacts."

I knew I should care that a huge deal just went bust along with a helluva a lot of money, but I didn't. Ashley would either find another deal, or she'd cave and sell just like me. It would work itself out. "I'm not sure how I feel about that."

"Let me know when you decide."

***

"I've been blackballed." Ashley hissed as she stepped into my office.

"Please, come in." I said dryly. I'd expected her to show up at some point, not that I was looking forward to it. I wanted her to pack up all of her things and disappear.

"The only companies interested in the proposal are out west or out of the country."

"And that displeases you?" Of course it displeased her. She wanted the cushy job at Steele. A job that would have at least kept her in the same circles with me.

"I wasn't planning to move to San Diego, but I guess I'll see what happens."

"You could always sell. It should be enough to get you out of whatever situation you're in."

She looked me up and down, "It would, but then what? I'm looking for a long term solution, not another Band-Aid. You know this isn't going to end for me. Besides, I'd go mad sitting on my thumbs without a job. Unlike you... what happened to you Jake? She made you soft."

"No," I replied calmly. "She gave me a life. It's something you may want to try, actually."

"Work is my life. It used to be yours. You have so

much potential and you're just wasting it here."

I sat back in my chair and studied her. She made me sad, there was so little to her life other than work and getting to the next prize. "I guess it depends on how you define potential. But you're right, I do have a lot of it. The projects we take on here are important and they matter to the people here in our community. And I have a helluva a lot of other potential in my life."

"You've got adoring husband covered."

"Thank you."

She smirked, "You really don't care what happens, do you?"

I shook my head. "Not in the slightest. The past is in the past and my life isn't about work, Ash. I keep telling you that."

She stood back up and moved toward my office door. "I understand, I just never thought you'd throw me under the bus." And with that dramatic statement, she left.

Chapter 31
~Eve~

I was just finishing up my day: shutting down my computer, making sure my files were straight, and reviewing my calendar for next week when my intercom buzzed.

"Yes?"

"We have an Ashley Grove here at the front. She isn't on your list. Should we let her in?"

I stopped dead in my tracks. "Team Blackball" (also known as Greg and Andrew) had worked fast, but I was still surprised Ashley had figured it out so quickly. "Yes, I'll be right up."

My adrenaline started pumping, surging through my veins and pounding in my temples. Greg said everything went perfectly on his end, and Andrew had gotten me the documents in record time. My entire plan was coming together exactly the way I wanted it to, but a little flicker of doubt kept flaring to life.

I was doing all of this behind Jake's back. Jake, who liked to be in control. I was essentially lying to my husband. While my plan felt so right, lying to Jake felt so wrong.

The offices were thinning out quickly, everyone eager to get to their weekend plans, so the halls were quiet as I made my way up front.

John, the security guard, was standing beside Ashley who was wearing a fresh visitor badge. She smiled tightly, "Thank you for seeing me."

"Of course. John, we'll be a few minutes in my office."

I waved for her to follow me. The walk back to my office was eerily quiet. I could feel her eyes watching me, studying my every move.

"Please, take a seat," I said as I closed the door.

She ignored me and stayed on her feet. "You've had me blackballed?"

I stopped only a couple of feet away from her and leaned in so I could speak as infuriatingly calmly as I wanted. "I told you not to cross my line. I warned you as plainly as I could what the consequences would be."

Her green eyes were on fire with an unchecked rage. The mask of Miss Sweet and Delicate was gone.

"You are insane, you know that? Who acts like this?"

I smiled at her sweetly, trying desperately to keep my own boiling anger from rising to the surface. "I do. My threats are never empty."

Her eyebrows shot up with surprise, "So, you are admitting to being insane? That's a new one."

I made my way around my desk.

Standing with the window at my back, I took a deep breath and explained as simply as I could. "Ashley, I told you then and I'll tell you again now... I protect the ones I love. That means doing whatever is necessary to keep them safe. I'd move heaven and earth for that man. If you want to call that insanity, then I'd love to be crazy."

"A simple conversation between Jake and I lead you to behave like *this*?" She sounded like she really thought I was crazy. Maybe I was. But I didn't know any other way to love Jake.

"Your simple conversation was actually very eye-opening for me. You showed your hand and I learned *exactly* who you are." I picked up the giant envelope sitting on my desk and tossed it at her like a Frisbee.

She caught it between her palms, her head jerking back and away. "What is this?" she asked, looking at it with disdain.

"You are done with Jake. You will sell The Nugget to the highest bidder and find a job somewhere other than the States. You will keep your phone calls and emails to business only until the deal closes, and then *poof*," I popped open all my fingers and swirled my hands in circle, "You will disappear."

"You can't defame and blackball me."

"I'm not doing anything illegal... yet. For some reason, every company on the Eastern seaboard called Greg last night wanting job references for you.

I can't help that he told them what you were like to your partners and coworkers. I can't help that he told them how you blew off an incredibly important business meeting to manipulate a former lover. None of that has anything to do with me."

She gazed at me through her lashes, one eyebrow arched as if she were bored with watching the crazy lady. "You think scaring off my job prospects will be enough to keep me from doing what I want?"

I finally sat down in my chair and leaned back, my eyes fixed squarely on hers the entire time. "I know that isn't enough for someone like you. People like you don't mind watching from the sidelines and waiting for a moment of weakness. Trust me; I know exactly how people like you work, Ashley. Open the envelope."

She flipped open the flap and pulled out the stack of papers and photographs. She blushed from her forehead to the first button of her blouse. She riffled through page after page and I waited, giving her several moments to absorb what she was looking at, to panic. "Did Jake tell you about this?"

"No. He's a good guy. He doesn't tell secrets."

She stared at the documents and photographs in her hands. Ashley was clearly in shock and I should have felt like a horrible person, but somehow, I couldn't muster the energy. "*You* are the one who kept insisting that you were the only one who could know Jake's dark side. All I had to do was find out what your dark side was."

Unfortunately for me, Jake was right. Now that I

knew Ashley had killed her own father to stop him from killing her mother, who then went and killed herself in front of Ashley anyway... I couldn't unsee the news articles and pictures Andrew had dug up. In a perfect world, I would have been much happier not knowing the details of Ashley's past.

But she hadn't taken no for an answer. She'd kept pushing the limits on a happily married man. I needed to know what I was working with if I was going to properly protect my marriage. I was trying very hard to not second-guess my decision.

Ashley finally looked up. Her hands were clenched around the papers and I could feel the hate. "What is it you want exactly? To ruin my life?"

"I don't want to ruin you, Ashley." I meant that. I may have gone lower than I'd ever gone in my life and just done something I may very well regret, but I didn't want to ruin another woman. "I just want us all to be on the same page. You seem to think you know Jake and me better than we know ourselves. And now, I know you, too. All the cards are on the table—no more secrets, no more lies." I leaned forward, "So this time, when I tell you to leave Jake alone, you really hear me."

She stared at me for a long time with those papers in her hands. Digging up Ashley's past, finding out all her dark secrets, and why she was so screwed up, had been a calculated risk.

"And if I'm a good girl this all stays between us?"

I nodded slowly. "You stay away from Jake and I won't breathe a word to anyone. But if I find out that one email or phone call was initiated by you without coming to me first, I will take that as your permission to take the gloves off." I smiled sweetly, "Fuck with my family again and you'll see what I can really do."

Ashley jammed the papers in the envelope and threw it back at me. "Fine. You have a deal." She was to the door before I could even stand up. "You won't hear from me again."

I was a strange mix of excited and miserable as I walked Ashley out of the building. I had her out of Jake's life, which was the most important thing to me, but I'd gone so low to do it.

I'd never thought of myself as someone who could so easily hurt someone else. This was going to take some time to get over.

I texted Greg as soon as I was back in my office, letting him know the final phase of my plan had been successful, then called my husband.

As the phone rang I felt giddy. It was like a huge weight had just been lifted off of our lives. I could float home on a cloud of my own excitement and worry about the consequences later.

"Hey darlin'," Jake's familiar drawl made my already pounding heart skip a beat.

"I'm just about to head home. Need anything?"

The line was quiet for a minute and I heard rustling. "Actually, I just got home from the grocery store. I was wondering if you were up for a surprise getaway this weekend?"

"Ummmm... ya. A weekend away with you sounds just about right. You must be reading my mind."

He chuckled, "You haven't heard my plan yet."

I didn't care what his plan was. It involved him.

I opened my drawer and yanked out my purse, frantically glancing around to make sure I had everything I needed before I left. "What is your plan, oh wise one?"

"I traded Andrew for the weekend, I'm sorry I didn't ask first."

"I really wish you'd warn me before you traded me to another man!" I teased back.

He groaned. "Hardly. He and Jennie were thinking of fishing anyway, so they were happy to have your boat instead."

"A weekend on the sailboat? Sounds... *awesome*."

"Agreed. So, we are stocked with food and drink, now I just need your fine ass to pack a bikini and we are out of here."

"I'm unlocking my car right now. Be home soon."

"Love you, darlin'. Drive safe."

"I will." I assured him as I tossed my bag into the passenger seat and started the engine.

Chapter 32
-Jake-

10 Weeks Later...

"Whatcha doing' under there cowboy?" Eve sounded playful but all I could see were her feet. I was under the Beast, changing her oil.

"Game over?"

"We won." She crouched down, bending her head so she could see me better.

"Congrats. You're in the playoff's then, right?"

"Yep." She got down on the ground and rolled onto her back. "It's been a long, long time since we've done this."

"Gotten dirty under the Orange Beast together?"

She nodded, but the look in her eyes was off. Eve looked like she was deep in thought. She was looking at me, but she wasn't *looking at me*. "Next month it'll be a year since you proposed."

That was a strange thing to bring up. "True. You thinking we need another vacation?"

She shrugged her shoulders. "Maybe. We haven't really gotten away since our honeymoon. It might be nice to disappear for a few days... just you and me."

I really didn't like the sound of her voice. Something was bothering Eve. "Let me get out from under here and we can talk, ok?"

Eve smiled, but it didn't quite reach her eyes. "I'll see you inside."

I quickly finished up and hurried in. Eve was sitting in her library reading in silence.

"What's up?"

She set the book aside and held up a large packet. "We need to talk about a few things."

I really, really didn't like the sound of that. I settled down on the opposite end of the couch so we could face each other.

"This packet is the final contract from Everlight Technology. Ashley has already signed everything and is good to go. They just need your signatures."

I took the packet. "Why did Greg give this to you?" There was absolutely no reason for Eve to be involved in any of this. The new deal with Everlight had come as a surprise about two weeks after the deal with Steele fell through. After another two months of walking through all the steps, everything was in place—including a new job for Ashley out in San Diego.

Eve took a deep breath and blew it out. "I haven't been completely honest with you."

You know that feeling of complete terror? How your skin feels hot and prickly a split second before your heart takes off racing and pounding in your ears? Yeah, that's how I was feeling right then. "Ok..."

"Greg and I are the reason the deal fell through with Steele."

And just like that my terror shifted straight over to rage. "You two did *what*?" I didn't mean to yell, but it came out before I could stop it.

Eve flinched and looked down at her hands. "I'm so sorry we went behind your back and I'm even more sorry I haven't been honest with you before now."

I felt like the rug had been yanked out from underneath me and I was lying on my back looking up at a strange ceiling. "Why?"

Eve's jaw flexed and her face flushed with anger. When she locked eyes with me I saw that hard determination I usually found incredibly arousing.

"She had to go."

"That wasn't your call." Greg I could see setting all this up, but Eve?

"You weren't getting rid of her. What was I supposed to do Jake? Sit around and watch her seduce you? Tear you down? Because that was what she was doing."

Suddenly I understood Eve's strange mood for the last couple of months. She'd been distant and unhappy. I thought it was just the lingering aftereffects of having Ashley in our lives. But now that I had all the information I realized it was much more than that.

"I can fight my own battles, Eve."

She shot to her feet and stuck a finger in my face. "That! That right there. *This* is why I did it. This is *our* marriage she was messing with. Yours *and* mine. It wasn't just your battle to fight and besides," she knelt down in front of me, taking my hands and looking up into my eyes. "We're a team. We fight together, Jake."

"Together? If this were a team effort you would have told me what you did sometime in the last two months."

She winced and looked down at her hands. "I'm so sorry. I didn't tell you because I..."

"You what?" I sounded angry because I *was* angry. I was fucking pissed.

"I was ashamed of myself, alright?" Eve stood back up and returned to the couch across from me. "I didn't know what else to do. She wasn't leaving and she was being awful. But I worried I went too far."

"So you didn't tell me?"

"I tried to make things right."

What did that mean? "Eve, I'm trying, really I am. But if you don't explain I'm going to walk out of here and cool off."

Her eyes went wide. "I had Greg find her a new deal. That was how Everlight came into the picture. He worked with Ashley to find her a situation that would work for whatever it was she needed. Everlight was ecstatic to get The Nugget and Ashley.

Greg put in a great word for her."

"So you just cut me out of the equation entirely? Thanks a lot, Eve." I stood up. I couldn't look at her. I knew she was trying to help and she'd done what she thought was right, but I couldn't hear those things. All I could hear were the lies and the lack of trust. The lack of faith in me. And that hurt like hell. "I'm taking a walk."

She didn't fight me, which I was glad for. I really needed a chance to think things through. I walked out to the yacht club and watched the sailboats bobbing in the water. The sun was sinking into the horizon and turning the sky bright orange. It reminded me of the night I gave Eve my necklace and journal.

We'd lived so much since that night.

I stared blankly, letting the anger eat away at me. I didn't want to think, but eventually the sun set and I was standing in the dark. The anger started to fade which made it was easier for me to sort through what I was feeling.

I hated that Eve kept something from me. Sure I was pissed she went behind my back, that felt weird, but ultimately I appreciated that she loved me enough to do what she thought was right. I'd eventually get over it.

But she lied to me. It just never occurred to me Eve could keep information like that from me.

I started walking back toward the house kicking every rock and branch that had the unfortunate luck of landing in my path. The lights were on in our bedroom and I could see Eve moving around inside. She was probably worried about me.

I'd been coming back to this house for so many years. We were basically still kids when she moved in. The parties and junk cars had been replaced by rising careers and renovations. It was a beautiful home and I wondered how it would change in another decade. Would there be bikes and balls lying forgotten in the grass after school? Drawings on the driveway and car seats in the car?

Ok, so I'd been keeping my own secrets from Eve. I hadn't brought up the kid thing once. Every time I talked myself into it, I chickened back out. This was the one time I didn't know how I would react to hearing "no". So instead I avoided it.

Was this what our marriage had already devolved into? Keeping things from each other and being afraid of talking about how we feel?

That wasn't what I wanted at all.

I marched into the house and up the stairs. Eve was standing in the middle of our bedroom with her jaw open. "Jake?"

"I want to have kids."

Her eyebrows shot up. Eve was probably expecting a diatribe on how mad I was, not a declaration of starting a family. "Kids?" she asked.

"Kids," I repeated. "Little ones that look like you and me, ideally. Or we can adopt if you prefer." Actually, adopting sounded like a fantastic idea.

Her mouth was still hanging open.

"Kids?" she repeated.

I took a step toward her and took her hand. "I know I said I'd never surprise you again, but I didn't know how else to say it."

She closed her mouth but she still looked stunned. "Where is this coming from? Is this a new way to end a fight?"

I grinned. "Nope. We can still fight if you want to. As I recall we're really good at makeup sex."

Eve nodded with a glint of mischief in her eyes. "Yes we are. You're not mad anymore?"

"Oh I'm good and pissed and we'll talk our way through this mess later, but right now I need to lay my cards on the table, too."

I took a deep breath. There was no reason to hold anything back; Eve wasn't running in the opposite direction. "Having a family is incredibly important to me. I never had one, not really. I want to give a kid what I wish I had. I want to be what I never got."

Her whole expression softened. "Oh."

"Is that a good 'oh' or a bad 'oh'?"

She put my hand on her hip and ran her free hand along my jaw. Our bodies connected for the first time all day. "A good 'oh'. I had no idea this was on your mind."

"What do you think?" I was holding my breath. I honestly had no idea where Eve stood on the whole idea of kids. She had two sisters so I always assumed she'd want a family, too. But maybe she didn't. Maybe that was the last thing she wanted...

She put both hands on my face and pulled me down for a soft kiss, then looked up into my eyes.

"Having kids scares the crap out of me. But my sister did it and Josh has Rosie and lived to tell the tale..."

"You are killing me Eve. What do you think?" I dipped down so we were on the same level.

She smiled and shrugged. "Kids mean a lot to you, huh?"

"I love you, Eve. I love you so much and that will never, ever change. If you say no, then sure, I'll be disappointed, but we'll move on. We always do. But yes, having a family of my own means a lot to me. I can't think of better way to erase my past than to make a future with a family I love."

She kissed me again and looked into my eyes. "Then I'm not so scared anymore."

I stood straight up. "Are you saying yes?"

She nodded slowly and tentatively. "Yes. I want to have a family with you, Jake."

I pulled her up into my arms and hugged the crap out of her. Then I took her to our bed.

"Jake! You silly man! I'm on birth control. I can't get pregnant now!"

"It's practice!" I laughed, kissing her.

"Practice, huh?"

I sat up, pulling her shirt over her head and unbuttoning her jeans. "Yep. We need lots and lots of practice."

She was as beautiful as ever. Not because she was sexy and amazing, but because I loved her and she loved me. I touched her skin, feeling the electric charge that always shot up my arm when we connected. What we had was unique.

"Jake," she whispered.

"Yes, darlin'?"

"I love you."

And that was the beginning and the end of everything.

Thank You

I hope you enjoyed Jake and Eve's story as much as I enjoyed writing it! I fell in love with these two and couldn't let them go with just one book. Next up in the series is Greg Hamilton, Jake's crass but loveable best friend. Look for **Book 3** in the Storm series in September 2014.

Connect with me online:
My website has everything: all the latest news, random articles, and updates on all my projects, including the First Draught chat series, Raising Awareness of Women in Writing (RAWWcon), and my upcoming action/adventure series The Unspoken Game. You can subscribe to my website or my very randomly issued newsletter at
www.alexisannebooks.com.

If you enjoyed reading Reflected in the Rain, I would appreciate it if you would help others enjoy this book, too.

Lend it. Share Jake and Eve with a friend.
Recommend it. Please help other readers find this book by recommending it to friends, discussion boards, or on social media.
Review it. Please tell other readers why you liked this book by reviewing it. If you do write a review, please send me an email at
alexisannebooks@gmail.com
so I can thank you with a personal email.
xoxo

Acknowledgements

I want to start by saying, "THANK YOU!" to everyone who has read my books. You have all been so supportive and made this insane journey so much fun.

Now, down to business. I can't say thank you enough to my writing group and to Romance Writers of America (RWA). When I took a chance and paid the fees to join, and then attend, the convention in Atlanta, I hoped to make it worthwhile. I had NO IDEA it would change my life. Those days in Atlanta I was submersed in what I can only describe as "home". An entire community of people who love to read and write books. Women empowering other women. Creativity celebrated, unleashed, and directed toward success. It was amazing, but that was only the beginning.

At the "First Timers" orientation I happened to sit down with Tracie Puckett, Lashell Collins, and Mary Chris Escobar—the beginning of the beginning of Write Club. We picked up Julia Kelly at the Contemporary Romance Ice Cream Social and never let her go.

In the months that followed, these ladies have changed my life through advice, encouragement, and example. And we're just getting started! Because of these ladies I'm continuing to meet new writers and industry professionals. I can't thank you guys enough!! Because of you, I learned to believe in my dreams. Belief is powerful. So thank you ladies, from the bottom of my eternally grateful heart.

I need to thank Jennifer Southard for being the best cheerleader ever, Tracie Puckett for cheerleading (and general Jake team support), and Julia Kelly for talking me out of lighting my manuscripts on fire. And for super CP powers.

P.S. Thank you to the sexiest editor on the face of the planet. I love you and those little super heroes we have running around our crazy house. LYWAMHASMM.

ABOUT THE AUTHOR

My pen name is Alexis Anne. I write romance, suspense, and sci-fi. I live in Central Florida with my sexy husband and our two little boy superheroes. I've lived in Florida my whole life and I would have no idea what it would feel like to live far away from a beach. I love the water, the sand, and the sun. I went to college to be an archaeologist, and that is exactly what I did with the first decade of my adult life.

I studied Anthropology and Classics at Florida State University (where I met my sexy husband) and then went on and got my master's degree in Applied Anthropology at The University of South Florida.

I love anthropology because it is the study of *us*. Whether I was a student or an oral historian, or an archaeologist, or a GIS specialist, I was working with people, studying their behavior, and their impact on society. I've always written, as a kid, as an academic, and now as a novelist.

My husband was in news until this past year. He's had some fun gigs—some I've gotten to tag along on, others I've just heard about. Now he's a mechanical engineer and finally using his giant math-genius for something useful.

We love music and would probably go to concerts every weekend if we didn't have kids, but we do, so we keep it to a handful a year. Right now we are on a monster Mumford and Sons kick (even got to go to the Gentlemen of the Road Stopover this year!) and we're so glad we got to see Imagine Dragons before they got super, crazy huge. We love to travel (a lot), and eat. Oh, and I also have a thing for reading. And an addiction to collecting books.

Books by Alexis Anne:

Filters: Polarized
Filters: Grayscale
Filters: Focus
The Storm Inside
Reflected in the Rain

www.alexisannebooks.com
alexisannebooks@gmail.com

Social Media:

Twitter: @AlexisAnneBooks
Facebook.com/AlexisAnneBooks
Instagram: @AlexisAnneAuthor
Tumblr: @AlexisAnneAuthor or
The Storm Inside Tumblr @TheStormInsideSeries

Be sure to sign up for my newsletter (on my website)!

www.ingramcontent.com/pod-product-compliance
Lightning Source LLC
Chambersburg PA
CBHW020235180626
46810CB00006B/2200